THE ROAD WINDS ON

THE
ROAD WINDS ON

By
Francena H. Arnold

MOODY PRESS
CHICAGO

Moody Press, a ministry of the Moody Bible Institute, is designed for education, evangelization and edification. If we may assist you in knowing more about Christ and the Christian life, please write us without obligation to: Moody Press, c/o MLM, Chicago, Illinois 60610.

Moody Giant Edition, 1970

ISBN: 0-8024-0066-3

Printed in the United States of America

To the young men and women
Whom I have learned to love in school and church
Who are now laboring in the harvest fields
All over the world,
For the love of Christ alone,
This book is dedicated

Contents

BOOK I

BOOK II

INTERLUDE

BOOK I

Chapter One

"Most ready, Half-pint?"

The small nurse at the desk looked up from the report she was filling out, and smiled at the young man who was leaning over the high counter that enclosed the tenth-floor office.

"Just a moment, Andy. I've got to take these down to Dr. Schaeffer. Then I'm through. I'll meet you at the elevator."

He watched her as she hurried down the hall, then turned to the white-haired woman at the desk.

"Does she never get tired, Waters? She never walks if she can run, and she'd never run if she could fly."

The older nurse laughed. "She's so full of the joy of living that she can hardly keep her feet on the ground. We're going to miss her when you take her away, Dr. Lewis."

"I need her worse than you do. Anyway, I spoke for her first," he said with a grin. "She's so little and so mighty! It's sort of invigorating to us jaded oldsters just to watch her swish those starchy white skirts down the hall. Her brothers and I used to call her Miss Biggety. Well, so long, Waters! We're off for dinner on a dune. Wish you could come along."

"You do *not*. And neither do I. I'm too old to enjoy my meals served up with sand and chiggers. And I'm smart enough not to want to be a third party when you and Kay are together on a moonlight drive. You just run along without me. I love you both, but not that much."

He was waiting when Kay stepped from the elevator, and they hurried down the hall and out the ambulance entrance.

Then hand in hand they ran down the block to the lot where the doctor's car was parked. Inside the shabby coupe he kissed her quickly before he started the engine.

"Hey, you!" she protested. "That's not allowed. We said no love-making when on duty."

"I'm off duty now, and so are you. And nobody saw us except those two draggled sparrows on the wire yonder. They look half-asleep and completely disinterested. Now, where do we go from here? We'll have to buy some makin's if we dine on a dune."

"To my apartment, Jeems! I have it all in the refrigerator. I bought it last night when Jan and I were shopping. There's everything there from soup to nuts."

"Let's leave the soup behind. It might present problems. And let's eat the nuts as we drive. I am so hungry I could eat turnip greens."

At the apartment which she shared with three other nurses, Kay packed the sandwiches, salad, and a small pie into a hamper while Andy filled the thermos jug with a cold drink, and washed and wrapped the grapes and peaches. Then they were back in the car, and in a few minutes were mingling with the traffic which rolled unceasingly along the broad drive. On their right rose the broken skyline of the busy city. On their left the lake sparkled in the late afternoon sunshine. Overhead the sky was blue, and a warm breeze came through the car window, tossing Kay's curls.

"My hair will be a mess by the time we get home," she said, brushing it from her eyes. "But I love it when the wind blows like this. And I love the lake when the sun is getting low and the little waves are dancing. And I love that love song you are whistling under your breath!"

"A love song? What was I whistling, miss? I'd really like to have you name it."

"I can't. I never heard it before. But it was a love song, I know. I could tell by its 'atmosphere.' Nothing but a love song could be so—so—poignantly sweet. Right?"

12

"I wasn't thinking of what I was doing, but I guess this was it, wasn't it?"

He whistled a few bars, and then at her nod of assent he said, "That is a love song, but not the kind you think. There aren't any English words to it, though I have often tried to write some. It is an expression of what Jesus in all His loveliness means to a black fellow who has been released from the power of the demons that had control of his life. David wrote it and you should hear him sing it!"

"It's beautiful, and before long I hope to hear him sing it. Oh, Andy, do you realize that in a couple of months, maybe before, we'll be there?"

"No, I can't realize it, though I go to sleep every night to dream of it, and wake up every morning to think of it all day long. Even while I was operating this morning the thought was still there. 'Kay and Dad, Kay and Dad.' I'm saying it in my subconscious mind, no matter what else I'm doing. Poor Dad is getting so tired waiting. The old house on the hill needs a woman's hand in it. He can't get used, though, to thinking of you as a woman. He still thinks of you as the thirteen-year-old he knew when he was home the last time. He's going to get a shock when you start running his lab."

"I shan't run anything," she protested. "I'll be just a nurse there, the same as I am at Brainard. Waters says a nurse's first duty is obedience. And when I'm on duty, the Drs. Lewis will find me a *most* obedient helper. When I'm off duty—"

"That's where the funny business will come in. You'll do as you please and make the Drs. Lewis like it!"

"Well, if they like it, so will I, and everybody will be happy."

"You said it! Happy! Happier than I thought I ever could be. You and Dad and I working together in the little mud-walled hospital. That is all the Heaven I want for a good many years."

The sun was fiery in the West, and the clouds about it were

13

ablaze when they spread their food on a cloth on the clean, white sand. As they ate, they chatted of affairs in the hospital, of their plans for the soon severance of that relationship, of the weeks of preparation that lay ahead, then a short period of deputation work for Andy while Kay went home to prepare for the wedding. That would be the last thing before they left, so that the ocean trip could be their honeymoon. They talked of the news from their homes, hers in the southern part of the state, and his on an African hilltop.

As they cleared the dishes and packed them in the hamper, Andy hummed again the haunting tune that had come from the heart of black David. Then they sat side by side on the sandy slope of the tallest dune and watched the moon rise over the lake. He told her again the things that lay close to his heart and his plans for their work together.

"Dad wrote last week that it will be the proudest day of his life when he can say to the waiting nurses, 'Dr. Andy will operate today.' I feel the same way about the day I hand over his daughter to receive his blessing. He will probably come to meet us and make the trip inland with us. We always enjoy the reactions of the newcomer to the sights and sounds of Africa. And to the smells! Africa has a smell all its own, and you'll never forget it."

"What are the sights and sounds that are so unique?"

"If we go by ship, we will have to make a long trip by boat up the river. And I mean *long*. You will begin to think that you are going to spend the rest of your life on that slow-moving stream. It seems to just slide along between the green banks. Sometimes it goes through deep forests where the trees hang low over the water, and the monkeys and birds chatter in the branches. And again it goes through the plains where the jungle grasses grow high and hide the animals that slink among them. Once in a while you'll see a snake festooned from a limb, or a hippo taking a bath. And always there's the hot sun by day and the deep, star-studded sky by night. It's wonderful!"

14

"It sounds thrilling! But if I get frightened by it all, you'll stay close, won't you?"

"So—o—o close like a leach. And Dad will be there, and David, as well as the boys that run the launch and do the cooking. I think Dad will bring Nellie Brady with him, too. In fact, next time I write I'll ask him to do that if she can arrange to be away at the same time he is. Then you won't be the only woman on board."

"Who is Nellie Brady?"

"Senior nurse. The only white nurse at the hospital. She's a honey! She must be older than Dad, and she's still going strong. She has trained all the other nurses on the staff. Some of the younger nurses were born there, and have come back twenty years later to help Nellie, and to train for service themselves. Oh, Nellie Brady is an institution there, one we couldn't operate without. She and David are essential, as essential as—as aspirin is to Dr. Clark!"

They both laughed as they thought of the jovial old physician who believed wholeheartedly in the virtues of aspirin. Then Kay returned to the questioning of which she never seemed to tire.

"How is David essential? Is he a nurse, too?"

"No, he's the hospital pastor. Maybe I should call him the chaplain. By the time we get up in the morning every day of the entire year, the patients are coming in. Some of them have walked miles through the jungle. They come down the paths leading to the hospital, some limping, some almost crawling, and some 'borne of four.' They have to wait their turn in orderly fashion. David sees to that. As they wait in the shade of the porch or under the trees, he reads Scripture to them. They love it. The ones who can't read are fascinated by the reading. And those who have been taught are proud as punch when David lets them read. Then he moves among them, telling the Gospel story, praying with them, bolstering up the courage of the frightened ones, 'doing the work of an evangelist' in his own way. And it's a great way! I believe

15

David has won more souls than any other worker on the station."

"Is he an old man?"

"About forty, I think. He was about eighteen when he was saved. I can barely remember it. He suffered a lot of persecution after that. His wife and two children died, poisoned we all thought. But we couldn't prove it. There's more poisoning done in Africa than anyone dreams of. The blacks know of and use poisons that the scientists and physicians have never heard about. Twice David was carried off into the jungle and tortured and left to die. But each time he managed to get back, and the last time he brought one of his captors with him—brought him back and won him to the Lord. He's a prince of a fellow, David is! He made that song the week after his wife died. It came, as my father once said, from a heart heavy with sorrow but glorying in sins forgiven. He has a grand-opera voice, and when he sings that song—"

Andy's voice broke as he drew in a long breath.

"You'll see them all soon, Kay—Nellie, David, Meteke, the blind evangelist, and Dad. You'll love them all, and boy, oh, boy! how they'll love you! Oh, you're going to have a grand time as a missionary, honey."

"I'm sure of that. I'll have a grand time any place as your wife, Andy. There's something else I was thinking about today. Are you *sure* we won't have to stop in Belgium? I do hope we can go right to the field."

"The way that has worked out is a modern miracle. Dr. Vansteenbergh spent an hour with the consul this morning. It looks like it's all clear. If I weren't African born, and if Dad were not so highly regarded, and if we hadn't studied tropical diseases under Dr. Van himself, and if we couldn't speak French, we'd have to go to Belgium. But all the red tape of three countries has been cut for our special benefit. I hope you appreciate that. And I hope also you appreciate all the hours I've spent teaching you to speak French as she is spoke! And as she is wrote!"

16

"I do appreciate all that. I think it is a modern miracle that the Board accepted me at all. And to get us through on this special toboggan, zooming us right past Belgium, is something extra special in the way of miracles. But the thing that is the biggest miracle and fills my mind to the near exclusion of anything else, is the fact that after loving you to distraction for eighteen years I've caught you at last, and you're really mine!"

"I sure am."

He stood up and drew her to him. He held her close for a minute, then they ran for the car. The real significance of her remark failed to register on his happy brain.

Chapter Two

A̲FTER LOVING YOU for eighteen
years."

The words sang themselves over and over in Andrew Lewis'
mind as he drove back to his room after leaving Kay at her
own door.

"After loving you for eighteen years."

Why, that would mean that she had loved him ever since
that day long ago when he had first met her and her brothers
in the front yard at Grandpa's farm. Could a six-year-old girl
give her love to a boy, and steadfastly maintain that devotion
for so many years? He doubted it, though he had to admit
that she had been his devoted, and often abused, little slave
from that first day.

What a funny little pigtailed mite she had been! And how
abashed he had been by her open championship of his cause
when her brothers had "ganged up" against him. He laughed
to himself as the whole incident returned to his memory from
the niche in his brain where it had lain hidden through the
intervening years.

He had been a very lonely little boy as he had perched on
the fence and watched Grandpa's two white roosters fight for
the supremacy of the barnyard. In the house Mother and
Grandma were doing the breakfast dishes and trying to tell
everything that had happened since they had last been together.
On the porch behind the screening trumpet vine, Dad and
Grandpa were sitting more quietly. Occasionally he could hear

their voices in conversation, but often there would be long intervals of silence. He guessed that Dad and Grandpa felt just as he and Dad did when they sat together on the porch at home and didn't talk. Folks didn't need to talk when each knew how the other felt—happy just to be together.

The only person who wasn't happy was himself. He didn't like this trip to America at all. He felt strange and uncomfortable on this farm which was not at all like the home in Africa. And he could not feel happy at being kissed and talked about by all these people who seemed to have the right to do it. Until yesterday Grandpa and Grandma and a lot of aunts and uncles had been in the same class as the people in his books, very interesting but very unreal. He had heard quotations from their letters, and at Christmases and birthdays there had been boxes with gifts in them. But he had never thought of them as real people like Dad and Mother and Nellie and David. He wished he and Mother and Daddy could go back quickly across the ocean to the safe home on the edge of the jungle where everything was nice and comfortable, and he knew all the people. He wished he could take off these new clothes and go out and play with Samuel in his old shorts and sneakers. He thought of what Daddy had told him when they left home—that they would be away a year and a half. How long was that? He wished he knew how many days there were left. They had been away a long time now. Was a year and a half much longer?

In his pocket were acorns he had picked up from under a tree in the yard. He wondered if he could hit the gatepost. One of his and Samuel's favorite games was tossing pebbles at a mark. He had better keep in practice so that he could beat Samuel when he got back. Hitting the gatepost had not proved easy. The acorns did not have enough weight to be good missiles. So he had slid from the fence, picked up a green apple that lay on the ground, and had thrown it with all his seven-year-old strength. To his amazement he had seen it land against the stomach of a boy about his own size. It could not have hurt much for, as Andy remembered it now, the boy wasted no time in self-commiseration, but immediately picked up the apple and threw it back, then both he and a larger boy reached for clods and prepared for battle. Andy had not meant to hit anyone. He had not seen the strangers as they came out of the woods across the road. Their sudden appearance, his chance hit, and their quick retaliation so surprised him that he stood in shocked immobility, realizing they were going to attack but he was helpless to defend himself. Then, quick as a flash, across the road darted a little pigtailed fury. She flung herself against him, turning to scream at the boys.

"Don't you hit him! Don't you dare hit him!"

"We will too! Get away from him!"

"I won't."

"Then we'll hit you!"

"No, you won't. You know what Daddy'd do if you did. Here he comes now!"

The boys had turned guiltily as she spoke, and when they saw their father come down the woods path, they dropped the clods and sauntered casually toward Andy and the little girl. Daddy had seen the man and had run down the steps to greet him joyfully, the way Andy felt he would greet David when they got back to Africa.

"Come here, boys," said the newcomer. "I want you to meet this fellow. You can call him your Uncle Tom, I guess. He's the chap I played most with when I was your age. These are my boys, Tom, and this disreputable-looking little hoyden is my only daughter."

Andy had been introduced, and then the four children had adjourned to the lot back of the big log building that Grandpa called "the old house." Here they prepared to continue the argument that had been interrupted.

"You shan't fight him!" Kay insisted. "It's not fair for two to fight one."

"Just don't you worry," Andy had insisted, wishing she

would mind her own business. "I can lick both of them if they'll come one at a time."

"What makes you think so?" bristled the bigger boy.

"I don't think so. I *know* so. You keep away till I lick him and then I'll lick you."

His heart was pounding and his hands were cold, but he would not back down now, and when his opponent approached him he met him halfway. He wondered now, almost twenty years later, how that fight would have come out. But he would never know, for it was stopped before it began. Again the little girl was between them, and although her brothers ordered her away with dire threats of what would happen to her when they got home, she maintained her stand, and the prospective combatants grew weary of arguing with her. The fight was given up in favor of a trip to the creek to catch "crawdads."

The year that had threatened to be long and lonely had flown as if on wings as the three boys had played together in the woods and along the creek, or trudged to the schoolhouse at the crossroads. America and Grandpa's farm had become places of high adventure, and Andy's erstwhile antagonists his inseparable companions and friends. Always with them, in spite of their pleadings and commands to the contrary, was Kay, her pigtails bobbing and her face flushed with the effort of keeping up.

They snubbed her, they bullied her, they tried bribing her. Nothing availed. She was always with them, and whenever possible, at Andy's side. He had felt pretty silly about it and wished she would go away and leave him alone. Harry and Ray had teased him and he had hated it. But nothing daunted Kay. Even at school she was his champion, in spite of the fact that he did not need or want a champion. At last he ceased to be disturbed, and accepted her as a necessary evil. She cried so hard the day he left that she became sick, and embarrassed him in front of all the grown-ups. He was almost glad to be going away to be rid of her.

It had been even worse on the next furlough. She had

been scrawny and freckle-faced, with braces on her teeth, and a mop of hair that always needed combing. He must have been more adroit in those days, for he often managed to evade her. There were times, however, when there were quarrels that he could still remember. He thought now, with a twinge of conscience, that it must have seemed hard to the girl to be continually left behind. All she wanted was to go along and enjoy the fun, and all that they wanted was to get away from her. Her mother usually had settled the argument, and a sulky, disappointed little girl had been kept at home. Andy felt remorseful over this memory. How could he ever not have wanted Kay with him? He would make it all up to her some day!

That was the last time Dad and Mother had been back to America. When next he came, he was entering college. Dad was alone in the house on the hill, and in the little cemetery where he had often helped cut the grass on the graves of the little brothers and sisters, there was a new grave where he and Dad had prayed together the night before he left.

He was a lonesome and homesick freshman that evening in September when he attended the reception for new students. He had reached America just in time for the opening of school and hadn't even seen Grandpa and Grandma yet. Somehow he didn't want to see them or go back to the farm where two happy furloughs had been spent. That part of his life was gone. Ahead of him stretched eight dreary years of study. He hadn't wanted to come. He had wanted to stay with Dad and let him teach him how to be a doctor.

It was silly that Dad, who was the best doctor in the world, should not be considered able to teach his son enough to enable him to practice with him there at the mission station. Rather than come off here he'd have chosen to stay on at the hospital and help in any way he could. Nellie Brady could have given him nurses' training, or he could have taught in the native schools. But neither the Board nor Dad would consider it. If he worked there, he must prepare. He was too old to stay on as a child. He must get ready for a man's life. So he had come. But his heart had stayed behind in the Congo.

He went through what seemed an endless reception line. He heard the names of the teachers under whom he would study. Then he was taken under the wing of an upperclassman and introduced to other newcomers. He hardly heard the names of either teachers or students, for his thoughts were too far away. At last, when the older youth turned for a moment to greet a friend, he seized the opportunity to escape from what was, to him, torture.

He slipped through a door and found himself out in the air, the warm, soft September that reminded him of evenings at home. He sat down on the top step and leaned against the pillar at his back. His lonesomeness and homesickness swept over him irresistibly. How *could* he endure it? It was a physical illness, a fever and a nausea that made him weak. All the grief he had felt at his mother's death swept back with intolerable ache. The separation from his father with its bitterness of feeling himself sent away from that beloved presence became a thing of poignant pain. He clenched his hands to try to still their shaking, but his teeth began to chatter, and he knew that he must get back to his room where he could be alone.

He had started to rise when the door behind him opened and there was the soft swish of long skirts across the porch.

"You're Andy Lewis, aren't you?" came a voice, low and a bit breathless as if its owner were nervous. "I saw you in there and thought I couldn't be mistaken. I've been looking for you."

"L—looking for me?" Who could be looking for him?

"Yes. I saw your name in the *News-caster* this morning. Pretty smart you are to get in the news the first week!"

He had noticed that the names of all students from foreign countries had been printed in the sheet, but he could not think who might be interested in him.

"You don't know me, do you?" the girl went on. "I'm Kay Putney!"

"Kay Putney!"

"None other."

"Miss Biggety?"

"Guilty."

"What are *you* doing here?" He started to laugh, then stopped and asked suspiciously, "How did you know I was coming here?"

"The conceit of you! I didn't know anything about you until I saw your name in the sheet. And I've just as much right here as you have. I'm going to college, Mr. Smarty."

"You—you aren't old enough."

"Oh, that's what *you* think."

"You're only sixteen. I know."

"Sure. Sixteen, but mighty smart! I skipped a grade."

"Teacher wanted to get rid of you?"

"Nope. Just so smart I was a hindrance to the rest of the class. So here I am."

She settled herself by him and went on to chatter of things down home. Gradually the tension seemed to go from him, and he leaned back in relaxation. He could not see her face, for the shade of the sugar maples by the walk held the porch in darkness. He wondered what the years could have done for her. She could have stood a lot of improvement, he thought, remembering the thin, freckle-faced girl who had made him miserable by her attentions.

"You see, I'm still chasing the boys," she laughed. "But I'm warning you now that this is the last time. Tonight is an exception. I promised Mom before I left home that I'd let the boys do the chasing."

"What if they don't chase?"

"I promised I'd still be a little lady."

"Humph!"

"How expressive! How complimentary! For that I'd like to bop you. But, being a lady, I can't."

"You chased me out here. Is that ladylike?"

"I told you tonight was an exception. You looked lonesome, and when I saw you sneak out I followed. I wanted to tell you how badly we all felt about your mother. I—I cried!"

"Thanks. She—she always liked you."

"She was sweet, and I know how you'll miss her. That's why I came out. I thought you'd be lonesome."

"I am—was."

"Thanks for changing the tense. That compliment offsets the other. It's the first one I've received since I came yesterday. Now won't you come in with me and get some of the best fruit punch you ever tasted. It's straight from Mt. Olympus, I think."

In the light of the reception room he stole a covert look at her and blinked twice to convince himself of reality. The years had indeed made a change. The freckles and braces were gone. Kay Putney was, he assured himself, easily the prettiest girl in the room. Later he amended that judgment to "in the school," and by the end of the first semester he confidently believed her the prettiest in the world.

At Christmas time he spent two weeks at the farm with Grandpa and Grandma, and renewed his friendship with Harry and Ray. For the first time since coming to college he really enjoyed himself. He began to believe that with Kay Putney in the same school, he might find his college years quite enjoyable after all.

All through the four years her friendship was a solid thing that he knew he could always depend on. There had been no talk or thought of a more serious relationship, for long ago he had decided that he would not marry an American girl and take her to the Congo. If he ever married he would choose one of the girls who came out to the field alone. There were plenty of them for, somehow, the young men seemed deaf to the call. He did not want to be responsible for what the Congo might do to a woman. Apparently Kay understood his attitude, for the friendship was a casual one on

25

both sides. Occasionally he had a mental picture of the future and Kay was at his side. But he put this away from him. She was a wonderful girl, a good friend, and he would always remember her. But she belonged in the gracious setting of a wealthy home in this land of plenty. He was dedicated to a needy place where life would always be hard.

It was pleasant, however, to have her here. And for four years they had studied and played together. Just a few weeks before commencement, the Foreign Missionary Fellowship had charge of chapel, and a veteran missionary who was having to retire because of approaching blindness, spoke to them of the needs of the mission fields of the world. Andy seemed to hear again his voice as he pleaded for volunteers to fill up the ranks on that battle front. His voice broke again and again as he told of the greatness of the need and the scarcity of workers. About twenty of the young people responded to the call, and the last one to go, when the old man had sat down and the choir was softly singing, "Anywhere with Jesus," was Kay—a subdued, white-faced Kay with tears streaming down her cheeks.

When they came out of chapel, Andy took her arm and led her down the walk, past the gym, and into the little park where the evergreen hedge hid them from view. They cut classes that day, but something more important than anthropology and science had to be considered between them. Even now, more than four years later, Dr. Andrew Lewis felt a thrill as he remembered that hour and how they knelt together for a few minutes by the park bench behind the shrubs before they went back to the world outside.

That summer Dad had refused to come home on furlough because there was no other doctor to take his place. It had been a good year on the farm, and Grandpa and Grandma had sent Andy back to Africa for a wonderful two months' visit. What a glorious time that had been! Dad's joy in his companionship was made greater by the knowledge that when Andy came the next time, Kay would be with him, and the

26

old house of sun-dried bricks would again have a mistress.

The next four years passed quickly to the young people. When one is in love, and the loved one is at hand, the time goes unnoted. To the tired, lonely doctor waiting in Africa and wondering if he would be there to greet them when they came, it was long. Kay had graduated from Brainard Hospital Nurses' School, and had stayed on for a year of laboratory work under Dr. Vansteenbergh, the Belgian specialist in tropical diseases. Andy had finished his medical course and interned at the same hospital. Brainard was the accepted medical center for several missionary boards, and always had on its staff one or two doctors who had served on a mission field. It was a highly regarded school for the training of young missionary doctors and nurses.

Now those years also were past. The future lay ahead, bright with promise. In a few months Dr. and Mrs. Andrew Lewis would sail for the Congo.

"That has a wonderful sound, 'Dr. and Mrs. Andrew Lewis,'" said Andy with a grin. "All right, Dad. Get the house ready. Dr. and Mrs. will be there before you know it!"

Chapter Three

WHEN KAY TOOK HER VACATION in late June, Andy went down to the farm for a week. It was the first time he had been there since he left college, for Grandma had died during his first year at medical school, and Grandpa was now living with Uncle Charlie in a suburb of the city, while another grandson ran the farm. It was a restful week with opportunity to be with Kay every day and to again have companionship with her family. The boys were married and living on nearby farms, and in each home Andy was made welcome with a sincerity that warmed his heart. Their wives were attractive young women, capably managing their homes and families and participating in all the activities of a busy community.

Those homes were a revelation to Andy. Grandpa's old farmhouse was, except for the electric lights that had been put in a year or so ago, and the oil stoves that had replaced the fireplaces as heaters, just as it had been built a hundred years ago. A well in the side yard and a cistern on the back porch furnished the water supply, and the water had to be carried in in buckets. A washbench with a roller towel on the wall beside it stood in the back entry. In the kitchen a wood-burning range served as heater and cook-stove in winter, while a small kerosene stove did duty in summer. Cousin Grace was not happy over the lack of conveniences that all her neighbors had, but she and Sid were just getting a start on the farm, and the necessary machinery must be bought before they could get anything for the house. Grandpa had promised that if this year's crops were good, he would do something for them. So Grace labored on and dreamed of a better day.

Andy liked the house the way it was, the way it had been when he and Dad and Mother came on that last visit. It seemed to have a strength about it that modern houses didn't have, as if it had partaken of the character of those who had given their strength in the making of this land. Nevertheless, he admired the shining perfection and the streamlined efficiency of the Putney homes, and wondered secretly how Kay would adapt to the life of a Congo housewife. None of the conveniences to which she had always been accustomed would be hers in that faraway home. He had not thought of that before, for the Congo was his birthplace, his dear home, and to his mind living conditions there were the norm. Now he began to realize the size of the sacrifice Kay would be making.

On a day when they went for a ride in the hills across the creek, he spoke to her about it.

"You haven't seen the way we live there, and you can't imagine the difference. Have I got the right to ask it of you?"

"Listen you!" she said indignantly, "in the first place, you didn't ask me to go to the Congo. I gave myself, and you can't interfere. And don't you think I know something about how you live? I've read every book about Africa that has been written in the last fifteen years. And I've talked to every missionary I could get hold of. And you've talked of nothing else. Don't you think I have any sense? I never expected to have a cabinet kitchen with hot water and a garbage disposal unit in my Congo home."

He chuckled. "Garbage disposal units you'll never miss, what with hungry blacks and the hungrier dogs. But you will miss your shower when you come in hot and sweaty and tired from a safari."

"Did the lack of those things bother your mother?"

"No, I don't think so, but—"

29

"But you think I can't take it as well as she did."

"No—o, not that. But Mom had never had modern conveniences in her own home. Farms didn't have them thirty years ago when Dad and Mom were married. In the second place, Mom came from a poor family and was used to doing without things that lots of her friends had. You've had everything, and you'll miss it."

"If I've had everything, it's time I learned to do without something. I'm no baby, Andy. And in spite of my name and my looks I'm not like the first Kate Putney."

"Oi, Oi! Was there another one? I thought I had the only one."

"Didn't you ever hear of her? Don't you know about her and the other Andrew Lewis?"

"No. Was there another one of him, too? This begins to be interesting. Did they get married?"

"You know they didn't, or at least you should. He was your great-great-great — I don't know how many greats — grandfather, and she was just as many great-aunts to me. Aren't you glad they didn't get married? Or are you? If they had, then you and I would be cousins of some sort and probably wouldn't be marrying. I never saw a cousin yet that I'd be willing to marry."

"In that case, then, I am grateful that they didn't fall for each other. Though how he could have helped it, I can't see!"

"Oh, but they did fall for each other. They loved each other very much and were engaged."

"Then why didn't they marry?"

"Because she wouldn't go to the mission field with him."

"But he didn't go himself. Grandpa told me it had been the dream of his life to see an Andrew Lewis go out. You know he was turned down because he was a cripple. What's the pitch about it all?"

"It's a good story, even if it shows up the Putney weak spots. Honest, Andy, don't you know it?"

"Cross my heart."

30

"Don't you know about your great-great-great-grandmother, Hester Lewis?"

"I've heard her name, that's all. Back home we didn't have time to talk about our ancestors."

"Well, she a tradition around here. It's strange your grandpa hasn't talked of her. She must have lived until he was grown. My grandmother remembers her well. The first Andrew Lewis was her son—and your grandfather's grandfather. And the first Katherine Putney almost was his grandmother."

"Why wasn't she if they loved each other? What gives?"

"She didn't have what it took. There are times when I think the Putneys lack moral fiber."

"One of them doesn't."

"Don't be too sure. I may disappoint you some day. I know lots of things about me that no one else except God, and probably the Devil, knows. I don't think very much of me."

"I do, and I don't think you will ever disappoint me. But come on. Tell me some more about Hester Lewis and the first Andy. What about his father? Wasn't he worth talking about? Why isn't he in the picture?"

"Probably because he died so long ago that he has been forgotten. But folks that are still living can remember her. She was a real character, if you can believe all that's been said about her."

"Hard-fisted old pioneer, was she?"

"No. Just a grand old saint. But a saint driving an old two-wheeled cart up into the hills alone at night when there was sickness, or going horseback if the roads were too hard for the cart. Or preaching a funeral if there was no preacher available. All the pioneer women, even the Putneys, knew what hard work in the house and fields was, but Hester added a few extra flourishes to the job of being a pioneer wife."

"That's fine, and I'm proud to be her grandson so many times removed. But what about Andrew and Kate? I'm more interested in them. And how did you know all this ancient history?"

"The year I was a senior in high school our class undertook a project of writing a history of the county. Did a mighty good job of it, too. It was multigraphed and sold all over the county, the proceeds going to the new athletic field. Boy, did we have fun! We went into attics and read old letters and newspapers and dug up things that had been forgotten a hundred years ago. Some of the stuff we could have used for blackmail. And some of it would have made you weep. Your grandpa let me rummage through all of Hester Lewis' stuff. It was rich! Then I found a box of old papers and letters in a trunk in our attic. I put two and two together and made—"

"Twenty-two out of them."

"No, just plain four. But I didn't give the story of Andrew and Kate to the editors. I wasn't too proud of the way Kate acted. Anyway it was strictly none of the other kids' business."

They had stopped on the summit of a long hill. They parked the car and went to stand looking back over the way they had come. They could see the road winding down the hill to the valley below. In the center of the valley was Grandpa's house, seemingly tucked under the trees around it. Farther away was the big white-columned home of the Putneys. Between the two was the stretch of woods where Andy and the young Putneys had played Indian, and the creek where they had fished. Through that woods ran a path that had been almost overgrown of late years, but which had been in active use this last week.

"This is a good place to tell the story," said Kay. "For in one letter that I found, one that Andrew had written to Kate when they were in the academy together, he spoke of their hilltop. Maybe this was it. Well, here it is. The story of the Putneys and the Lewises began about one hundred and twenty-five years ago, I think. I'm not too sure about the dates, but I should think it would take at least that long to become the great-great-great-grandparent of a big goof like you. Thomas Lewis and Henry Putney came out here when the country was opened by the government. They settled on

32

those two farms and built homes, and then went back and got their brides. Sarah Putney was the 'grand lady' of the community, but it was Hester Lewis that made her mark on it."

"I'm beginning to remember her. Grandpa has talked of her, but I didn't pay much attention. She didn't seem real. I think that perhaps I haven't been too attentive when Grandpa gets to reminiscing."

"You've missed some good stories, I'm sure. She must have had awfully bad luck with her children, for there's about a half-dozen tiny graves on the lot by her and Thomas in the cemetery up there by the church. Andrew must have been the only one to live to grow up. And he was engaged to the Putney daughter, Katherine."

"And it busted up, somehow?"

"Exactly. *That* part of the story I read in some old letters Kate wrote to her mother when she was visiting an aunt. I got a bit here and two bits there and pieced them together. I'm not sure of all the details, but I think that just before they were to be married, he felt a call to the foreign mission field. He must have felt a great urgency, for missions in those days were pretty primitive stuff if what I've read of them is true. Anyway, Kate didn't share his call. In fact, she thought he was crazy, and told him so. The engagement was off. That's when she went to visit her aunt.

"Then after all, Andrew didn't go. His father was hurt and was an invalid for the rest of his life. I *think* that when Kate heard it, she came back expecting to get him again. But he had other ideas. Guess he didn't want a woman who went back on him when the going began to look hard. You know now what a slacker the first Kate Putney was. If she *had* gone, she would probably have whined all the way because she got her velvet and lace gowns all mussed up. We have a picture of her dressed up like a Christmas tree!"

"What does it look like?"

"Somewhat like the Kay Putney of the present clan."

"She must have been lovely."

"She was a spoiled brat, I'm sure. And as I said when we got onto this subect, I may have the name and the looks, but I surely hope I've got more starch in my backbone!"

"Freckle-face, starch is one thing you've never lacked. But you've got something better too. You've got the love of Christ in your heart, and the longing to share Him with the world. I think that was what Mistress Kate lacked."

Kay was silent, and her face was thoughtfully pensive as they drove back down into the valley. Andy did not notice her unusual silence. The drowsy summer afternoon was conducive to quiet. He drove slowly, musing on his good fortune to be engaged to the Katherine Putney who had strength and character enough to be willing to go to the heart of the Congo jungle with her man.

Chapter Four

THE ANNUAL MISSIONARY conference was in progress at the Fulton Street Church a few blocks from Brainard Memorial Hospital. Andy and Kay attended whenever they could get away from their duties. Thursday was devoted to the Congo work, and they spent the entire day at the meeting. Several of the missionaries were known to Andy, two of them from the Board under which his father served. Kay listened eagerly to the conversations and thrilled with anticipation of the time when she would be a part of this fascinating work.

One veteran nurse held her audience for an hour as she recounted story after story of the triumphs and tragedies of the work in the mud-walled hospital where she had labored for over forty years. She had gone out as a young woman, and had laid her entire life—its hopes and dreams, its talents and strength—on the altar for the Lord and her beloved blacks in the heart of the dark continent. Now she was back in America facing retirement that was harder to be borne than her labors had ever been.

"If the Board would permit me, I would go back tomorrow and serve until the Lord calls me home. But that cannot be. So, as long as I am able, I will go about on deputation work and try to give out a message so compelling that young men and women will answer the challenge and go forth to serve in that rich harvest field. Oh, I am almost moved to envy them! Just to be able to go back and serve!"

35

Her voice broke, and Kay's eyes glistened with sympathetic tears. Then the speaker went on.

"That would be wonderful! But there is one way of life that is better, the most wonderful thing of all. That is to leave all one's ways in the nail-pierced hand of the Master, and to know that whether He says, 'Go,' or 'Stay,' it is all right. Just to go where He wants me to go, just to be what He wants me to be."

She sat down amid a breathless silence. Kay reached for Andy's hand and held it tensely, her breath coming quiveringly.

During the lunch hour, Andy was so busy greeting friends and making new acquaintances, that he would have forgotten to eat had not Kay reminded him. He found a table where a group of Congo missionaries on furlough were dining, and sat listening hungrily to their conversation as he ate. Kay could not understand all the references to things that lay outside her experience, but she listened intently and thought, "Someday Andy and I, with our children maybe, will be coming home on furlough. We'll have to attend conferences like this, too. That will be great! But Andy will have to do the speaking. I'll *never* be up to that!"

As they went back to the afternoon session, Andy was exhilarated, talking almost feverishly.

"Let's hurry, Half-pint. I want to get a seat where I won't miss even an inflection of the speakers' voices. This meeting today has made me more homesick than I have been since that first week at college. There's a big difference, though. Then it made me despondent because the time ahead was so long. Now I'm all up in the clouds because the time is getting short. Dad seems so near today that I can almost hear his voice. I keep wanting to answer back, 'Here we come!' "

The afternoon session was further inspiration, and on the stimulus of it Kay felt that the weeks of delay that lay ahead were needless hindrances to their progress toward their goal. But it was the evening program that gave the crowning touch to the day. One of the Board members had toured the stations and had brought back pictures that would tell the story of progress better than any words could. These were shown, and for an hour and a half the audience forgot America, and rode and walked through the forests and jungle paths of Africa, or watched with keenest interest and sympathy the work in hospitals and schools. At the last there were pictures of the missionaries in their homes, smiling and waving greetings to the ones who were holding the ropes back home.

Kay watched it all, noting that the houses were commodious and homelike with vines and flowers in profusion. One interior showed a living-room with radio, easy chairs, rugs, and lamps. It could well have come from any section of America. She drew in a long breath of satisfaction. Even though she would not admit it to Andy, there had been a drawing back from the living conditions she feared she must face. As the only daughter of prosperous parents her life had been easy, and she loved the beauty and comfort of her home. She wondered how she could adjust to the lack of them. But if these scenes were typical, she need not fear.

The scene on the screen at the moment was the most attractive one that had been shown, a rambling house under great branching trees. A broad veranda with easy chairs looked shady and inviting. Kay heard Andy catch his breath, but she did not recognize the smiling man who waved from the steps, until Andy, apparently forgetting where he was, burst out, "Oh, that's it! Our house! Hi ya, Dad! We're coming!"

A ripple of laughter went over the crowd, but it was sympathetic laughter. Most of them had discovered that Dr. Tom Lewis' son was in the audience, and they enjoyed his enthusiasm. After the close of the service as the young people drove to Kay's apartment Andy was jubilantly happy. To him, going to the field meant going home. He was not alert to the fact that to Kay it would mean leaving all that was familiar and dear to her and facing the future among strange and, at times, terrifying circumstances. Kay, herself, gave this no thought. She had no thought of other circumstances when she was with Andy.

All of the next day they were kept busy. The Brainard Hospital Staff worked in co-operation with several of the missionary boards, and the medical examinations of the candidates and returning missionaries were given there. Andy was one of the examining physicians, and Kay was in the laboratory. There was no opportunity to attend the conference until evening. All day Kay had worked under the influence of the previous day's emotions. She was thrilled to be a part of this great adventure, the real battle front of Christianity. To be in the van of that army at Andy's side seemed to her to be the culmination of all that she could desire.

They entered the meeting late. A film was being shown, of what field they did not know, and it was too dark to read their programs. On the screen they saw groups of children playing happily about the huts that were their homes. Their smiles showed unusually white, even teeth. Then young people and adults were shown. These were smiling also, but the smiles seemed only silly grins, for all the teeth were gone. The empty gums gave even the young girls the appearance of senility. Kay shuddered at the sight of them.

A voice spoke in explanation. "Their religion demands that they have their teeth filed completely away when they are ten years old. All during childhood the children look forward to the time when this ceremony can take place, for that marks them as adults. An adult with teeth is an outcast. I stood with my camera in hand for over two hours while a little girl endured this ordeal. Only my determination to let American Christians know of this cruel and futile practice kept me there through the waves of nausea that almost overcame me. Oh, that we who claim Christ as our own would show such devotion to our faith!"

On the screen the picture that the camera had faithfully recorded unrolled before their eyes. On the ground lay a beautiful little girl, her hands and arms held down on each side by a stalwart man. The third man, a priest of the tribe apparently, leaned over her, filing rapidly and vigorously at the teeth which had gleamed so whitely a short time before. She made no outcry, although the watchers in that audience grew sick at the sight. An occasional convulsive movement of her arms or hands was the only sign she gave of the excruciating pain she was enduring.

Kay stared at the screen in horror. As a nurse she had seen some repellent and sickening things, and had grown inured to them. But this was a form of torture so exquisite in its keenness that she felt she could not watch it. Yet she could not turn away. She bit her lips until she tasted blood. Andy glanced at her anxiously, but could not see her clearly in the dimness. He could hear her, as well as many others around him, gasp as the operator of the crude file grew more vicious in his efforts. Still there was no outcry from the pitiful little figure on the ground.

At last it was over and the girl was raised to her feet. For a full minute she stood facing the camera, the blood streaming from her mouth and down the front of her dress. A woman was heard to murmur in amazement, "Why, she's not even crying!"

But Andy, being a doctor, knew what that immobile face and expressionless eyes meant. And Kay whispered hysterically, "Look at her eyes, Andy! She's in shock."

The picture continued, showing other people and other scenes, but Kay sat as if unable to lift her head. When it was finished, she said, "Let's go, Andy I want to get home."

They left quickly, and it was only when they were in the car that she spoke.

"I'll see that picture all the rest of my life!" she cried. "It was just *too* awful. I can't believe it's true. Nobody could be so senseless and so cruel!"

"It was terrible, honey. But I'm sure it was a true picture of what the missionary saw happen. I've heard of such ceremonies. Paganism *is* senseless and cruel, all of it. You have to see it to know *how* senseless and cruel."

"Do they have such things as *that* in the Congo?"

"Not that, no. But they have other practices that aren't pretty. I shan't tell you about them now. There will be plenty of time for that later. Our job just now is to get through all the passport, visa, and medical hocus-pocus. The mumbo-jumbo will come after we get to Africa."

She smiled at him, but her eyes were troubled. After he had left her at her apartment, she stood by the window watching until his car had been lost to sight in the boulevard traffic. As she turned away, she whispered, "Oh, Andy, Andy, I love you so much I'd die for you. I hope you will never doubt that, no matter what happens. And I hope you'll always love me. Sometimes I wonder if a Putney is worth it!"

Chapter Five

Both KAY AND ANDY were on duty all day Saturday so had the evening free. They drove out into the country to the Farm Kitchen, where they had discovered a cook who could fry chicken "as it should be fried." Kay seemed unusually quiet, but Andy did not mind. He knew she had had a hard day, and he knew also how she liked to ride without talking and just enjoy the sunsets in the open country. Being a child of the hills, she had never seen a sunset spread out across the full horizon until she came to this prairie city, and she had never ceased to enjoy it.

After a wearisome day she loved to relax and absorb the beauty of the ever-changing sky. That suited his own mood tonight, for his mind was busy with the events of the day. He had performed a tonsillectomy that morning on a temperamental child with a bad heart. He had spent most of the day with the little patient and his parents, and had only come away after seeing him asleep, with another doctor in charge. He, himself, would go back for a final check before going to bed.

Being a doctor was the best thing a man could do—that is, being a missionary doctor. And surgery was the best part of it. There was always a thrill to him to know that with the sure, clean cut of the knife he could right some wrong, or rid the body of diseased tissue that medicine could not cure. He thought of the "blue baby" that Dr. Hirsch had operated on yesterday, and of the almost hysterical joy of the parents when they had seen the pink flush steal into the cheeks of the little

41

one. He saw again the look on the face of the Domato boy when he learned that he could eventually play baseball again. His throat constricted as he remembered how a young mother had leaned over and kissed the foot of her baby when the cast was taken off and she saw it straight and strong instead of the malformed club it had been.

"If Grandpa had had such treatment, he might have been cured. Then he, too, could have gone to the field."

Even when things went wrong, it was great to have tried, to have given one's best strength and ability in an effort to meet the need, to know that all had been done that could be done, and the results left in the hands of the great Physician who could heal or refrain from healing as His loving will decreed. Oh, it was great to be a doctor, especially a missionary doctor who was almost ready to go back home after eight years of exile here, and who would be taking back with him the best gift, aside from salvation itself, that God ever gave a man— a devoted and loyal wife who would share with him the labors and the heartaches, the joys and the rich harvest of the years ahead.

They drove into the lane that led to the Farm Kitchen and parked under a tree. In the gloom of its thick shade Andy turned to kiss Kay, saying in concern,

"Why so sober, Half-pint? Not feeling well?"

"Oh, I'm o.k. Just thinking."

"Does it hurt so much?"

"Yes, sometimes it does," with a nervous laugh. "I guess this quiet country atmosphere is conducive to introspection."

"What language! Where did *you* learn such big words? If that's what thinking gets you, I'd advise an immediate operation. Cut it out!"

"Okay, doctor, no more thoughts for a whole hour."

They found a table in an alcove that had been an understair closet before the farmhouse had been remodeled. It was just large enough for two, and they enjoyed the seclusion it afforded away from the noise and distractions of the main dining room.

While they waited for their orders, Andy drew from his pocket and unfolded on the table a large sheet of paper.

"Look what I did one night last week when I was so pepped up over the prospect of going home that I couldn't sleep. I got out of bed and made this drawing of the hospital and the new wing we are going to build. Dad wrote a few weeks ago that they have all the bricks made so we can start building as soon as he and you and I get together on the plans. I think we can hustle things up a bit by making some tentative plans and sending them on to Dad. He can revise and amend and send them back. By the time we've fitted his suggestions into ours it will probably be time for us to sail. We could be all ready to start laying bricks as soon as we get there. Are you a good bricklayer, Half-pint?"

"Probably as good or better than you."

"A well-spoken truth. But you will have to be *much* better to be of any value as a mason."

"Who *does* lay the bricks? Surely there aren't many of the natives who are skilled."

"On the old building Dad did a lot of it himself. Even when the natives did the labor he had to be continuously on hand to direct them. They have no idea of the value of the straight line, and no interest at all in following a blueprint. When they were left alone, the results looked like a game of dominoes with lines rambling off in every direction. But things are lots better now. There is a group of educated fellows that can be used. Two or three of them have finished what is the equivalent of our high school. Lots of the young men and women are going into the cities to work, and though they usually don't stay long, they bring back new ideas. Even those who have attended only the bush schools have a lot of practical experience, and will do a reasonably good job under strict supervision. Dad won't have to be a day laborer this time—nor will you."

"That's reassuring. But how *could* your Dad do all that

43

and tend to his sick folks too? Who ran the clinic and dispensary while he was building?"

"Oh, he ran them both, he and Nellie and Mother. I never thought much of it at the time—I was only six when they finished the hospital—but now I wonder how he stood it. I've heard Nellie tell about one day when he had six major operations in that little hut that was the first hospital, besides countless numbers of such things as cleaning ulcers, opening boils, washing out infected eyes and the like. And then he went out and worked on the hospital for several hours."

"That shouldn't have been. What did your mother say?"

"Oh, she'd try to get him to rest. But when he wouldn't she and I would go out and carry bricks for him."

"She shouldn't have."

"I know that, but she did it anyway. I suspect that three-fourths of what has been accomplished on the mission field was done by folks who were, by all the standards of common sense, completely out of bounds."

Kay was gazing at him soberly, and now she asked in a troubled voice, "Does it always have to be so?"

"I wouldn't say it *has* to be. I just say it is. If all Christians were in there pitching, some on the field and some at home, preaching, teaching, giving, praying, we could get the job done in short order. But it isn't that way. And while some folks loaf on the job, others work too hard."

"Yes, and some die. Your mother did."

"Yes. She would probably be living now had she stayed in America. But Dad told me once that they knew what they were facing when they went. They took a calculated risk, as businessmen say."

"You had some brothers and sisters who died, didn't you?"

"Two of each. Before we got the big kerosene refrigerator, it was awfully hard on white babies. The food didn't agree with them and it spoiled quickly and—say, why all the questions? You aren't worried are you, honey? It isn't like that now."

44

"I was just wondering."

"Just wondering! Just thinking! Something's troubling you. You'd better confess. Oh, oh, here's our dinner. Now we'll 'just eat.' "

As they ate, Andy led the conversation into impersonal channels, watching Kay closely for signs of preoccupation. Whenever a few minutes of quietness came, her face would betray again the fact that her thoughts were troubled. But when, as they were again in the car ready for the trip homeward, he questioned anxiously, she gave only an evasive answer and began to talk of the beauty of the night.

"Let's put the top of the car down so we can see the stars," she suggested.

"Okay, but if I do any stargazing we will have to find a place to park. I can't keep my eyes on the stars and the road at the same time."

Already her mood had changed. "I've no time for it anyway. I have to be on duty at seven, and you have to catch a few winks of sleep before you have to get up. Isn't tomorrow the day you are to speak in the Huntington church?"

"Sure 'nuff. Guess I won't see you again until Monday."

"Then let's enjoy tonight."

As they drove cityward, she was unusually vivacious, chatting of doings in the laboratory, telling of the jokes they played on Dr. Schaeffer, and recounting the news from home.

Andy enjoyed it all, glad to see that her troubles had been forgotten. But before he slept as he reviewed the events of the evening, there was something in even that hour to trouble him. He could not decide just what it was nor why he should be disturbed by it, but neither could he shake off the uneasy doubt that assailed him. What was wrong? He tried to reconstruct the evening and decided that she had been very tired after an unusually hard day in the laboratory. After the supper with its rest and relaxation, she had felt so refreshed that she just had to bubble over. He was drifting off into

45

sleep when, unbidden and unexplained, a memory came of a long-ago day on the farm.

He and the three Putney youngsters had been returning from the woods where they had buried old Sport, the dog who had been the playmate and companion of the Putneys as long as they could remember. It had been a shock to find him dead in the shed, and even the boys had cried. Kay had been inconsolable, and had wept so tempestuously that her mother had told her that if she did not become quiet, she would have to go to bed while the boys buried Sport. She had choked down her sobs then and stood by while they wrapped the old dog in a piece of canvas and placed him on their wagon, but while the boys dug the grave, she had sobbed again with her arms around her old playmate. She had sat on the wagon hiding her face in her lap while they filled the grave and placed a pile of stones on top of it.

They had all started back to the house soberly and sadly, and were trudging through the pasture back of the barn when Kay reached over and slapped Harry on the wrist.

"You're it!" she cried, "and you can't catch me."

She was off like a flash with Harry in pursuit. Andy and Ray watched the race and cheered when she was almost caught in the orchard. By the time Harry reached that spot, however, she had climbed a tree and was stocked with enough green apple ammunition to keep all three boys away. She was coaxed down to make a fourth in a game of croquet and was so impish that the boys were soon laughing hilariously at her tricks.

"Is she crazy?" asked Andy of Ray as they stood together at a wicket. "She howled like everything about Sport. And she's forgotten about him already."

"You don't know Kay," said Ray. "I guess she must be a *little* crazy, but she hasn't forgotten about Sport. She'll most likely cry herself to sleep tonight. Just now she's puttin' on an act to make us think she don't care. When she puts on an act, she makes it a good one!"

Ah, that was the answer! Kay, many years later, was putting on an act again—an act designed to make him think she was not disturbed about something that really was troubling her very much. What *could* it be? Monday he would find out. He had a right to know and to share her troubles.

But when he looked into the laboratory Monday morning to wave the greeting he always gave her, she was not there.

"Jan came past to report that Kay was ill," volunteered the nurse on duty. "Said she was awake all night and was going to try to sleep all day."

He went to the floor where Jan, Kay's roommate was on duty but learned no more.

"All I know is that she said she couldn't sleep because of a terrible headache. I gave her some medicine, and she was trying to sleep when I left. Said she didn't want to be disturbed."

"I'm going over. She might be really sick. I want to know."

"Better not. You know Kay. When she says don't disturb, that is what she means. Wait until I get off duty and go with me. She won't die in the meantime."

When they reached the apartment at four o'clock, however, it was empty. A note was propped against a bowl on the table.

Dear Jan,

I am going to catch the afternoon train for home. I called Walters and fixed it up. My headache is better, but I feel rotten and want to go home and be fussed over by Mom. Tell Andy I'll write a letter to him. I don't know when I'll be back.

Kay

P.S. Tell Andy *please* not to telephone. The letter will explain everything.—K.

47

Chapter Six

IT WAS THREE DAYS before the promised letter came. Andy was tempted to call, but realized that the better way would be to respect Kay's prohibition. Nevertheless, he was much disturbed, and the waiting time dragged. He knew now that some very real problem was troubling her. It was not a matter primarily of a headache or any other physical ailment. She would have told him freely about that. It was deeper, and intuitively he knew that it concerned him also. Was it something that had come up as a hindrance to their going to Africa?

The only thing he could think of was that her parents, who had never really liked the idea, had in some way made an appeal that had been strong enough to win her over. Perhaps they had played upon the fact that she was an only daughter and owed a loyalty to them that forbade such a separation. He knew it would have to be some tremendous pressure that would effect a change in her attitude, for he had been in the Putney home the night Kay had told her parents of her engagement and her intention of going to the mission field with Andy. He had heard their pleas, had listened to their arguments, and had seen their tears. And through it all he had seen Kay, white-faced and tearful, but resolute.

"I *do* love you, Mom and Dad. Please don't talk that way. I love you so much that I ache all over. But I *have* to do this. It's my job! And I won't be alone. Andy will be with me, and much as I love you both, he comes first. That's God's plan, too. Try to understand. *Please* do."

They had tried, and through the years they had offered no further opposition, although they let it be known that they still hoped something would intervene to change her mind. Had they, as the time drew nearer, made their yearning over her so evident that she had been convinced that her duty lay with them? He could not believe such a thing possible, yet no other explanation came to him.

The letter was waiting in his room when he came in after a day that had dragged unbelievably. He was tired and discouraged and full of doubts. He had hoped all day that the letter would come, yet when it lay before him he dreaded to open it. He had convinced himself by this time that any news in it would be bad. He sat down in his one easy chair and opened the envelope with hands that shook. As he read the pages and the full impact of the words came home to him, his heart grew sick within him.

> Dear Andy,
>
> Oh, you *are* dear, dearer than I can ever make you understand, and much more than you will believe after you read this letter. For I am going to hurt you terribly, darling. I'd rather be hurt all the rest of my life myself than to give you one minute of pain. And yet I have to do it, and all the lifetime of suffering that lies ahead of me can't assuage the pain of knowing I have hurt you.
>
> I am not going to Africa with you, Andy. There, it is out! I wondered if I could ever write it. I've thought and prayed, and cried and prayed, until I'm sick and weak. But I can't make it come out any other way. I know you will never be able to understand why, for any girl who loves a man as much as I love you ought to be willing to follow him to Timbuktu (that's in Africa, isn't it?). And I would, Andy, if that were all of it. But when I explain, you'll see that's *not* all of it. I'll try to make you see the whole thing.
>
> In the first place, please don't blame Mom and Dad.

They didn't know anything about it until I walked in on them this morning after catching a ride out with the mailman. They are distressed over the whole situation. They'd like to be happy about the fact that I won't be leaving them, but they feel so bad over my treatment of you, that they're all upset. They can't understand my decision *not* to go any better than they have ever understood my decision *to* go. Just now they are probably thinking of my pioneer forebears, Henry and Sarah of one hundred years ago, and sympathizing with them over their temperamental daughter. They think Kate and I (were, are) a couple of cowards.

I *am* afraid, Andy, but it goes a lot deeper than that. If that were all, I would force myself to go. Of course, I'd be a complete flop after I got there, but my love for you would carry me along for awhile. But I *can't* go, Andy, cross my heart.

I guess it all started when we began to get things ready. Buying clothes for years ahead, listening to Dr. Vansteenbergh discuss all those tropical diseases with you—diseases we never hear of in America—talking with Mr. Barnes about visas and the other red tape, made it all real to me for the first time. I started to feel very reluctant about it all. At first I assumed that was the way all prospective missionaries felt. You would not know about that, for you were born on the field. Then I began to hate the things that I'd hear about what the missionary nurses had to do. Some of the letters I had read were pretty awful, and made me feel sort of curdly inside! When I was with you and you talked of your home and your dad and David, I would feel all right. Then I'd hear something else that would upset my balance again.

Once I went with a visiting nurse to help her take care of a colored family that had measles. I just hated it, Andy. The smell was awful, and they were all so dirty, I couldn't stand them. I went home and lay awake all night turning things over in my mind. If measles smelled like that in America, what would they be like in African huts with no sanitary facilities at all? I almost told you the next day

50

that I couldn't go through with it. But I didn't, and the next evening we went to the dunes and you sang that lovely song David sang, and I convinced myself that a people who could produce a David must be a joy to work with. Then came the conference, and after the first day, I went home thrilled and in the clouds again.

But the next night we saw that *awful* film. You didn't know it, Andy, but I had my eyes shut through most of that. I just couldn't look. When I opened them and saw that poor youngster with that look of shock, I almost passed out. Even after I was at home and in bed, I could not forget it, and Saturday night I couldn't think of anything else.

I wasn't fibbing when I told Jan I had a headache. I really did have a headache and a heartache too, for I knew this thing meant sorrow for both of us. All night long I had lain awake, thinking and arguing with myself. Even though you had assured me that your tribes had no such customs, I knew that I would run into other things that would frighten and sicken me. I tried to reassure myself by saying that I would not be afraid of anything when you were with me, but at last I had to admit defeat. I believe I love you as much as any woman could love a man, but that doesn't seem to be enough.

After Jan left for the hospital I got up and tried to read, but I couldn't sit still. I walked the floor and cried. I wanted to send for you, Andy, but I didn't dare. I knew I had to fight it out alone. I thought it would get better, but it didn't. It got worse, and I heard myself saying over and over, "I can't do it! I can't do it! Even for the sake of Andy Lewis, I can't do it."

How many times I said that, I don't know, but suddenly the enormity of it hit me like a thunderbolt. Right *there* was where the trouble lay. I was planning to go to Africa for your sake and not for the sake of those poor folks who'd never heard the Gospel—and this is worst of all— not even for Christ's sake. Just to be with you.

I sat down in my big chair, Andy, and saw the whole thing clearly for the first time. I went over it all, from that day in chapel when I volunteered for foreign service until now. I tried to be absolutely honest. The answer I got to every question was just this. Unconsciously perhaps, but nevertheless in reality, I had worked up an interest in missionary service in general and in the Congo in particular because you were going there. The same old game I'd been playing since the first day I saw you—girl chase boy.

I am going to be decent and honest about it at last. I guess I'm just like the first Kate Putney after all, for I'm not going to Africa with my man. Perhaps someday I'll grow tall enough and broad enough in Christian grace to hope that you will find as good a mate as Andrew did, and that your descendants will number among them men as fine as you are, and women as good as she. As yet, however, I haven't got past the place of hoping you never marry. *I* don't intend to. I'm feeling sorry for Kate, and I will never speak scornfully of her again. I can understand now how she could love Andrew more than she could express, and yet not be big enough to measure up to his standard of womanhood.

This one thing else is clear to me. I know that I've never felt the least bit of a "call." I believe the only call that could come to a Christian and send him forth on such a task as that would have to come through a more complete devotion to Christ than I am capable of. He alone is a sufficient compulsion. If one loved Him enough—as much as you love Him, Andy—he could go any place and not be afraid. But I don't measure up. So I am trying to do the hardest thing of which I am capable. I'm letting you go without me, without trying at all to hold you.

Please don't try to see me, Andy, nor write to me until you have accepted this verdict. I couldn't stand an argument. Mom and I are going to visit some aunts, and I am not coming back to work until after I hear that you have sailed. It is better that way. Wherever you go my prayers will follow you. And for the last time, let me say it, I do love you, Andy.

Kay

52

The letter slid from his hand and the pages scattered on the floor, but he did not notice. For a few minutes he sat as if stunned, then his arms were on the table and his head bowed on them. How long he sat thus he never knew. Sometimes he prayed, but more often he struggled with the questions and doubts that kept intruding. It did not occur to him to try to see Kay or change her decision. She had made it after deliberate thought and prayer, and no one could change her. She had asked him not to see her, and he knew she meant it that way. He would respect her desire.

The prospect before him was a dark and lonely one. The weeks before he sailed, which had seemed so full of happy preparation, now stretched ahead desolately. The work of assembling his outfit, instead of being the pleasant experience he and Kay had planned, would be bitter drudgery. The trip across would be a time of sad relinquishment, rather than the honeymoon he had anticipated. When he met Dad and David, it would not be to present to them his bride, but to tell them the story of his loss.

It seemed to him that he could not wait to see Dad. He felt as he had the night after Mother died. He wanted to feel Dad's arms around him and to weep on Dad's shoulder. Only there could he find comfort for this sorrow that had come upon him. He had to get to Dad as quickly as possible. He would go to the office of the Board tomorrow and get them to hurry things through. He would not wait for a ship. He would fly on the first plane he could get after his visa came. Maybe in a couple of weeks he could make it. He could not endure the thought of a longer wait. Just now he was not Dr. Andrew Lewis, physician and surgeon. He was just Andy Lewis with a broken heart, and he needed his dad!

Chapter Seven

Mr. BARNES at the office of the Board listened sympathetically as Andy stated his case in blunt and unequivocal terms. He was going out alone, and he wanted to start as soon as it could be arranged. Miss Putney was not going, either with or without him. How soon could it be arranged for him to leave?

Mr. Barnes was shocked and at a loss to express his sympathy to one so evidently desirous of evading any such expression.

"I am sorrier than I can tell you," he said when Andy had finished, "but if she has been mistaken in her leading, it is better for her to discover it now than after she had arrived on the field. I can understand your desire to leave as soon as possible, and we will do all that we can to help you. Your passport is okay, and the visa should come through soon. If your outfit is ready, you can go as soon as we get plane reservation after that. You get everything lined up and we will let you know."

For a week his days and nights were full, so full that he allowed himself only the minimum of rest. Why go to bed anyway, when he couldn't sleep? More and more, as he kept his thoughts from dwelling on Kay, he found them turning to Africa and his father. He dared not think of what he had lost, Kay with her gay charm and her forthright facing of any issue, and most of all, her unashamed love for him; so he reminded himself, instead, of Dad's gentle kindness, his sympathetic understanding of the sorrows of others, his undaunted courage in the face of seemingly insurmountable difficulties. In the hours when he worked at the hospital or at his packing he seemed to feel Dad's presence with him, steadying his hand in the operating room or approving the compact tidiness of the packing cases. And at night when sleep would not come and Kay's smile and her long-lashed blue eyes kept intruding on his vision, he seemed to hear the deep sad voice as it had spoken that last morning they were together.

"Oh, my son, God bless you and keep you, love you and guide you, and bring you safely back to Africa in His good time!"

As his father had a furnished house waiting for him, there did not need to be the large quantity of household equipment that the new missionary usually has to take on his first trip. With none of the wedding gifts and bric-a-brac that would have inevitably attached themselves to Kay, the packing was not difficult. There was his treasured X-ray machine, the instruments that he had bought at the sacrifice of many a needed garment, the books, his projector and cameras, and a new microscope for Dad. At Uncle Charlie's where Grandpa lived, a new station wagon, the gift of a host of relatives, waited in the garage. It was not a great array of goods, but it meant a more effective ministry. That was all that mattered.

At the end of ten days the phone call came while he was in surgery. "Come to the Board office as soon as possible," the message said.

As he waited for the elevator in the office building, he found himself whistling for the first time in two weeks. He was still lonely for Kay, he had an ache in his chest that wouldn't go away. But he could whistle, for he was going home. Back to Africa and Dad! He pushed open the door and stepped into the outer office. Usually he stopped here to joke with the girls who were working here, typing, filing, bookkeeping. Today the desks were empty and the machines silent. Funny for them all to be out at the same time, away from the phones. The doors to both private offices were closed, but he did not stop to knock. He had been sent for, so Mr. Barnes must be expecting him.

His rubber-soled shoes had made no noise in the outer room, and when he opened the door Mr. Barnes sprang to his feet as if startled. For a minute he stared in confusion at Andy, then without a greeting came across the floor to lay one arm around the young man's shoulder while his hand convulsively clasped the one that had been put out as if to ward off a blow. He struggled to say something, but it was not necessary. Andy knew from the reddened eyes and the white face. He straightened his shoulders and asked huskily, "It's Dad, isn't it?"

Mr. Barnes nodded and reached for the cablegram that was open on his desk. It was short. Missionaries do not have money for long cablegrams.

"TOM LEWIS WITH THE LORD TODAY. ALLISON."

Yes, with the Lord, with Mother and Grandmother, with those other children who had lived such a little time that their father had had no companionship with them on earth. Probably he was playing with them now—he and Mother and those four little ones together. And he, Andy, was here alone with no one to care.

That seemed all he could think of. He ought to do something and not just stand here like a lump of lead. He ought to say something. But all he could think of was that Dad was gone, and he was left alone. Mr. Barnes tightened his arm and found his voice at last.

"Sit down here, Andy, and let me get you some water. I wish there were something that I could say that could help you now. It's such a shock to all of us."

"I—I think I'd better go to my room."

"Don't go, fellow. Come home with me. Mrs. Barnes will want you. Come on. I'll leave now."

"No. No, please. I want to be alone."

"I wish—don't you think it would be better—"

"I'll be all right. Please don't worry. I just want to be alone tonight. I'll go to Grandpa in the morning. Don't tell him in the meantime. I should be the one to do it. Let me have it my way."

Alone in the little room, crowded now with packing boxes and piles of equipment, he sat down in the big chair and let the full realization of his loss flood him. In this same spot two weeks before he had thought his cup of pain was full. He had faced life without Kay and found it dark indeed. But he had had Dad then, and had planned to be with him in a few weeks. And all the time he had felt Dad's sympathy and strength, the comfort that Dad had always been in any need that arose. When other people or things failed him, he had always turned to Dad. Now there was no Dad to turn to. He was alone.

He prayed, but the words seemed empty and meaningless and no comfort came. He tried again, as he had in the office when he first knew his Dad was gone, to think of him rested and happy with his other dear ones in Heaven. But all he could see was a new grave in a little Congo plot, a place that had probably become weed-grown with Dad so busy and he so far away. Or he saw the lonely brick house on the hill, with a few black servants going sadly about. Their singing would be stilled, he thought. For them, as for him, the shadows would be very dark just now.

As he dwelt on this picture, he thought of the happy preparations that had been made for his return to them. Dad had written of the sweeping and garnishing that was going on to get the place ready for the young doctor and his bride. The letter telling that he would be alone had not reached them yet. He had delayed sending it because he had dreaded to put into words the story of Kay's defection. It had been sent only three days ago and would not yet have arrived. Dad had been spared that disappointment.

His thoughts kept turning toward that home which was now

empty. It would still stand there in the African sunshine, even though the animating spirit of its owner had gone. Samuel and Rebecca, the caretakers, would be there, for they had no other home, and the missionaries would keep them on to hold the house and grounds in readiness for the young doctor's return. And David would be there, David the faithful and loyal, David who had been as a dear brother to him. His heart, too, would be heavy and lonesome tonight. Oh, to eliminate the miles and be back there with him! Together they would kneel and pray. With David's arm across his shoulders he could get through to God and be able to see the light behind the shadows that now crowded so thickly about him.

He looked about the room at the boxes all tagged and ready for shipment. All that was lacking was the visa. Oh, if it would only come soon! Then the truck would take away all this stuff, and he could grab his luggage and be off on the first plane that would take him. No honeymoon ship and slow river trip for him now. Roy Allison would meet him at the airport with his light plane, and in a few days he'd be home! Maybe there he could convince himself that Dad was really gone. Maybe when David, and Nellie, the Allisons, and the others told him how it came about, it would become a reality. Now it was an unpleasant dream.

If only Kay were here! But he put that thought away as quickly as it came. No need to reopen any other wounds tonight. One, raw and bleeding, held all he could bear of pain.

Chapter Eight

AT MIDNIGHT, chilled by a cold wind that came in off the lake, Andy arose to close the window. In the dim light of the street lamps outside he noticed a letter on the table, where his landlady always put his mail. Even in the dusk of the room he knew whence that thin airmail letter had come. Shakingly he turned on the lamp by his chair and with fingers clumsy and cold reached for the letter opener. He shut his eyes for a moment against the pain that the familiar scrawled writing brought with it, then he drew a long breath and began to read.

Dear Son:

I am very tired and lonely for you tonight.

This will be a short letter. It has been a hard day. I lost two patients on the table. If I were in America, I would tremble for my reputation. Both of them were hopeless cases when I started. All one can do is his best. There will of course be rumblings from the insurrectionists who are always with us. They will convince some of the natives that I have a devil. Sometimes I wonder if I should refuse to operate when the end is a foregone conclusion. But because once in a blue moon one of the hopeless ones lives in spite of everything, I never have been able to refuse a case. God may be the only one who knows I've done my best, but He does!

I can hardly sleep nights for thinking that before long you will be home and there will once more be a woman's voice in these quiet rooms. And in a few years, God willing, there will be small feet running over the floors again. I wonder if I will live to see that. Like Paul I am pulled two ways. I'd like to see your children growing up around you. Life is easier for children in the Congo now than it was a generation ago. But, on the other hand, to depart and be with Jesus and my other dear ones would be a glorious thing. So whatever comes will be glory because it is His will and He will be with me.

The grumblings and rumblings among the natives grow daily. This past week has been bad. There have been several clashes, with shooting in the nearby villages, and so many deaths by poison that it cannot be accidental. The unrest in the south is spreading, and the troublemakers have enlisted the co-operation of the witch doctors. There is a new fetish worship, too, that has won a large following. Many of our weaker Christians have been led away. The last time we had a baptismal service each of the twenty-three families represented suffered a death or serious illness inside a week. We know, of course, that it didn't "just happen," but to prove it to these frightened and credulous folk is a different thing.

I think I could face all this more confidently and courageously were it not for David. Somehow it never occurred to me that he could be affected. But for a week he has been unusually quiet, no laughing or singing at all. When I have wanted him, he has not been at hand, and when he returns from these mysterious absences he is unresponsive and almost surly. I was concerned for him, but did not doubt him until this evening just at dusk I saw him and two other men slip away into the jungle. I had been to the hut of a sick man and was returning alone. They did not know that I saw them nor did they see me. One of the men was the old medicine man's wicked son who is a leader among the troublemakers. The other was a complete stranger, an evil-looking chap. David was going along willingly. They were ahead of him and he was going along purposefully. I have sat here until one o'clock praying for him, but he has not returned.

If David has deserted us that seems more than I can bear.

Since you have been away, he has been my greatest comfort. I am praying that my fears are groundless and that morning will bring a happy solution to it all, but just now the night is very dark.

I will be ashamed after I have mailed this letter for having burdened you with these things at a time when you are so happily planning your new life. But we promised to share our problems, and you are a son of Africa and must carry her burdens.

I will write again, perhaps tomorrow as you will want to know about David. But pray, son, pray.

Your loving Dad.

The letter dropped from Andy's hands as the shock of those last few paragraphs made him weak. David! The one he had called his big brother, who had been the companion of his childhood, who had taught him the lore of the jungle and forest, and who had ever set him an example of consecrated Christian living amid all the temptations that the convert from heathenism has to face. David, who had carried his load on the long treks when he would otherwise have had to be left behind. David, who had eaten with him, slept with him, prayed with him. How terribly strong the evil forces out there must be to have conquered David!

They had conquered Dad too. No doubt it was because of David's fall that Dad's overtaxed heart had failed. He thought of the lonely white-haired man sitting all night waiting for the return of the fellow he had loved as a son. And he pictured the defeat of the cold, mist-shrouded morning that failed to bring back the wanderer. No wonder Dad couldn't take it. If David was a failure, whom *could* he trust?

Suddenly, with a revulsion so strong that it shuddered through his whole body, Andy Lewis knew he was not going to Africa; that he hated Africa and everything connected with it. Africa had been cruel to him and he owed it nothing. He had lost to it his mother, father, brothers, and sisters. He had lost the best friend he ever had, and the lovely girl he was sure God had given him as his mate. He had done enough for Africa. He did not want to see the old home again. He hoped he would never *think* again of the filthy grass-roofed huts, the children with their sore eyes and running ulcers, the whining leprous old men and women. He wanted to wash from his mind the sights and sounds and smells that stood for Africa.

If, after all the years of missionary effort, after the unselfish living and giving of men and women like Mother and Dad and the Allisons and hundreds of others, those stupid black people wanted to remain in their dirt and ignorance and sin, he would not disturb them. He shuddered again at the thought. If a man like David could forget his years of clean Christian living and crawl back into the mire, any efforts to help him were futile, and a waste of human energy and love. He was done with it!

He sat, sick of soul and body, all through that night. Sometimes he thought of his father, and burned with anger at the memory of what he had sacrificed and suffered. He thought bitterly of David and of all that Dad had done for him since the day he came as a sick and hungry seeker after the white man's truth. The bitterness increased as hour after hour he brought up out of his memory the years of his father's service— the long safaris into the jungle, stopping at each dim, half-hidden path to serve the people who were gathered to meet him, the days beginning at dawn and going on until midnight when he had operated for hour after hour then, without rest, had turned to the task of building.

There was never a minute to read a book (and how Dad loved to read!) or even to play with the little son who, whenever possible, tagged his footsteps. Not even time to indulge in grief when his wife died. Andy winced and groaned now, remembering that a half-hour after Mother had been buried Dad had performed an emergency appendectomy. And after all that, he was deserted and left alone, waiting for the one who did not come, for the prodigal who preferred the husks of witchcraft to the feasts of the Father's table. Let the prodigal eat with the swine then. He, Andrew Lewis, was through!

Kay had been right after all. She had been quicker than he to see that it was not worth the cost of the lives that had been poured into it.

At the thought of Kay his pulse quickened. The barrier between them was gone! He could go to her now. She, of all the people in the world would understand how he felt. No—he couldn't go now. He didn't know where she was. He would have to write and have her father forward it to her. In the meantime he must go to Grandpa and tell him about Dad. He wouldn't say anything about his change of plans to anyone, not even to Grandpa or Mr. Barnes. Kay should know it first. The others could wait. If he told them now, they would think he was just unsettled by Dad's death. He knew that wasn't true. He knew that he never should have considered the career of a missionary. What he would do he did not know. That decision must be discussed with Kay. It, too, could wait.

Tomorrow he would go to Grandpa and try to comfort him in the loss of a beloved son. Perhaps he could get some crumb of comfort himself. He and Grandpa needed each other now.

Chapter Nine

ANDY SAT IN THE SWING on the side porch of his uncle's suburban home, watching Grandpa as he read his morning mail. He noticed with a feeling of pain that the last few days seemed to have added years to the old man's looks. The shoulders seemed more bent, the walk more feeble. The missionary son had been a great source of pride and joy to the man who had been turned down for such service himself because of a malformed foot. The infirmity had not kept Grandpa from a life of action and hard work on the farm, but two Boards had considered it a sufficient hindrance to keep him from the mission field. So the son who had gone had seemed to be his representative.

Andy knew that almost all of Dad's support had come from Grandpa and the aunts and uncles. He thought with a feeling of dread of the ordeal he must go through soon, that of telling Grandpa that he, Dr. Andrew Lewis, was not going to pick up and carry on the torch that had been dropped. It would not be easy, but it had to be done, and as soon as he heard from Kay he would tell the whole sad story and get it over with.

Grandpa looked up from the letter he was reading and asked wistfully, "How'd you like to drive down to the farm for a few days, Andy?"

"Okay. Are you going?"

"I'd like to if you'll drive me down. Charlie'd raise Ned if I tried it alone. Sid writes that Grace and the children are going to her mother's for three weeks, and he thinks that would be a fine time to get the work done we've been plannin'. He'd like to have it done as a surprise for Grace's birthday."

"What is the work?"

"Goin' to have the kitchen made modern, sink, gas range and all, and a bath put in where the little hall bedroom is upstairs. Think we'll put in a lavatory downstairs, too. That big old pantry could spare a chunk easy as not. Then a couple of little floor furnaces put in. I promised I'd pay for the materials if Sid would get the work done. It's kind of a slack time now with the corn laid by and the wheat harvested. Sid and the Putney boys will do the work. They claim they can do it in three weeks and I'm willing to be shown. You wouldn't mind drivin' me down, would you?"

"No, if you want me to."

"Maybe you could stay awhile yourself. Can you spare the time?"

"Yes. I told them at the hospital that I'd be gone indefinitely."

"Tell you what we'll do, boy. We'll drive your station wagon down. It's over in the garage behind Charlie's store. He's had it out several times to limber it up a bit. A trip like this is just what it needs."

Andy did not answer. What could he say to the old man who had been planning for seven years to give a car to his missionary grandson? What would become of the car? Certainly he would not accept it now, even if the folks did not withdraw their offer. Surely the Board could find someone else who needed it, some other young couple who had not yet been disillusioned.

Grandpa, having read the letter from the grandson who was running the farm, turned his attention to the other envelopes in his lap.

"Nothing but ads and requests for money. I'd like to know how every auto dealer and investment broker and even every fur-storage house in the country got hold of my name," he grumbled querulously. "And all the crazy isms that have ever been known want money from me. I don't have a fur coat. Never did and never will. Yet here are two firms fallin' all over each other in their desire to store it for me. Who gives 'em my name?"

Andy laughed. "That's just modern advertising, Grandpa. I got a letter the other day asking for the privilege of storing my wife's jewels. Having neither wife nor jewels I filed it in the wastebasket."

"Well, I wish they wouldn't send them. It's such a waste of money. I feel sort of guilty at getting so much mail and never doing anything with it. But all the money I can spare from bare living goes where it will count for more than buying a fur coat for an old codger that can stay by the fire when it gets cold."

"Don't worry a bit about it. That cost is all counted in as a necessary expense. And their idea of a necessary expense is a bit different from yours. If all Christians were as conscientious as you are, there would be no lack of money for any good work."

"And if all young people were as yielded to God's will as you are there would be no shortage of man power."

Andy winced but did not answer, and Grandpa went on with his reading.

The three hundred miles that stretched between the city and the farm was a pleasant drive of varying scenery. At first, after the suburbs had been left behind, there were the dairy farms with their well-painted houses, big barns, and rolling pasture lands. The cornfields were rippling green seas between broad stretches of stubble that had, a few days before, been sinuous waves of golden wheat. Grandpa leaned back restfully in the station wagon and gave a great sigh of relaxation.

"I like your drivin', Andy. Charlie gives me the heebie-jeebies. I don't know why he thinks he has to get every place day before yesterday. I'll stay home any day before riding with anyone of his youngsters. They aren't wild or bad. They're just geared to this age and I'm out of gear to it.

You go just right to get there eventually and enjoy the scenery along the way."

"Thanks. I hope you do enjoy this ride. If I forget and go too fast just you call me for it and I'll behave. You like to be going back to the farm, don't you?"

"Yes and no. It's home and no other place ever will be. I didn't want to leave after your grandma died, but the boys wouldn't hear of me livin' alone. I couldn't run the farm any more, and Sid was lookin' for a place. So I let him have it. I do get homesick for the old neighborhood, but when I get there and your grandma isn't there I have to go through losin' her all over again. You don't know yet what it means to have your life so fused with another that when that other is gone you are only a piece of a person. That's one reason I can't grieve too much for your father. He is so much better off now, that to grieve would be sin."

"How can one help it?"

"Guess we can't help grievin' a bit, and the Lord won't blame us for that. He wept over Lazarus. But a Christian can't let his life be made morbid or his effectiveness ruined by it. Your father never wrote me a letter after your mother died without mentioning her. He missed her all the time like he would have missed an arm. But he kept on working until he was called to join her. I am not fit for much work any more, but I don't aim to sit around whittlin'. I'll keep busy, even if it's only wipin' dishes for my daughter-in-law. But I do get lonesome."

"Then you come back to the farm because you're homesick, and when you get there you're still homesick. Isn't that it?"

"Yes. It's good to talk to someone who understands."

"That's the way I felt when I went back home the year I graduated. I was homesick, but without Mother things just didn't seem right. But Dad was there and I got used to it. If you had stayed on at the farm, you would have become accustomed to the loss."

"I guess you're right. You'll have the same battle to fight

when you get to Africa. Now with me, I don't have to meet that about your father. He seems closer to me now than he did in Africa. I *will* miss his letters though."

Andy did not answer. When Grandpa referred to his return to Africa, he felt uncomfortable, as if he were cheating the old man in some way. If only Kay would write so that he could tell folks of his change in plans and get this secrecy over with. Of course the letter had hardly reached her yet, so the answer would not come for many days. Did time ever move so slowly?

Grandpa was talking again. "I get homesick for the old church, too. Charlie's church is all right. I like the preacher, and the people are nice. But I'm not a part of it. I have never felt at home like I do in the old church."

"It's a great old church, isn't it?"

"It sure is. Did you know your great-great-great-grand-parents built it?"

"I remember Dad mentioning it once. We were building a new church on the field and the old church sent a hundred dollars to help. Dad said that, if he remembered rightly, that was the tenth mission church that the old church had helped to pay for."

"That's right. He wrote me about it at the same time, and your grandma and I counted up. Since then Don Morgan out in India has built another, and his sister Jean and her husband have built one in Burma."

Andy was having a hard time keeping his thoughts on his grandfather's rambling words, but he was determined to keep the conversation away from himself, so he asked, "You said my great-great-great-grandparents built that church. Do you mean they actually constructed the building?"

"Not all of it. The Sunday school rooms were built much later. And we just put in the basement about ten years ago. But the main building was actually built by Henry Putney and Sam Morgan and Thomas Lewis—and their wives."

"Did the women help with the labor?"

"Indeed they did. I've heard Hester Lewis tell about it many a time. Oh, those pioneer women could work!"

"Do you remember her? Why, she must have lived more than a hundred years ago!"

"She did. But she didn't die until after your father was born. I can remember her yet, holding him in her arms as she sat in her old rocker. Sure I remember her. Do you forget, young man, that I am a great deal nearer to one hundred myself than I am to your age?"

"From what I hear of her she was quite a character. There wasn't much went on in the community that she didn't start, was there?"

"Guess you're right. She *was* a character. After her son Andrew died she raised my father and his brother and sister. Their mother lived only a few years after their father went. So the only grandparent I knew was Grandmother Hester. I used to think that she would never die. I didn't see how the world could keep on running without her. I used to stand in awe of her, but I liked her immensely."

"How old was she?"

"Past ninety-five, I believe. Can't remember exactly. And she was still chipper as could be. My father used to say that no matter what happened Grandma Hester never bowed her shoulders nor dragged her heels. When she died, she went quickly. It was just as if she knew it was time to go, so she went! That was the way she did everything, with no delay."

"Do you remember your great-grandfather, too?"

"Oh, no. He and my grandfather both died when my father was just a youngster, the time of the big typhoid epidemic. That was just after the Civil War, I think. Grandma Hester was a widow for over thirty years. That's a long time to be lonesome," he added sadly.

Andy wondered how many years there were ahead for him to live in lonesomeness. Didn't one ever get over it?

The day was warm and the sun made a glare on the pavement ahead of them. When he saw Grandpa's eyes close against the brightness, Andy concentrated on his driving and soon a gentle snore told him that the tired old man was asleep. That would eliminate for awhile the likelihood of embarrassing questions. It was good to drift lazily along in this shimmering summer sunshine and let his thoughts lie dormant for awhile. There were issues to be faced he knew, and problems to be solved, but just now he wanted to push them all aside and exist in this state of suspended meditation.

Noon came and passed, and he thought longingly of a hamburger, but not until Grandpa opened his eyes and sat up, looking sheepishly about, did he consider stopping.

"You lazy rascal," he said with a laugh. "You've been asleep two hours. You probably laid awake all night thinking about getting back to the cows and the pigs and the old oaken bucket."

"Well, if I did, I didn't make anybody walk the floor with me as you did the first night you ever spent at my house. Hey! it's after one, and I'm hungry. Aren't you plannin' to stop till we get home?"

"I was just waiting for you. There's a town coming up. Rub those eyes and get ready for hamburgers!"

They had been climbing gradually toward the hills, and when they drove out onto the highway after eating, Grandpa gave a happy sigh and pointed ahead of them to the haze-covered trees that seemed to stand against the sky.

"The hills of home!"

Everything he saw now reminded him of some long-ago happening or of some well-remembered and beloved scene. The sun became overcast and erelong the rain came down in a gray drizzle. Andy's thoughts took a quick trip to the depths of an African forest, and to a time more than twenty years ago when he had been on a trip through the villages with his parents. A hard rain had come up. David and another man had hurriedly contrived a little box-like shelter which was large enough for him and Mother to sit in. It was covered with canvas and hung from poles which were carried on the men's shoulders. He remembered how cozy he had felt in the dry little nest, with the rain beating on the canvas and with the splash of the bare, black feet outside. There was the same feeling now in spite of the stretch of thousands of miles and what seemed an eon of time. This was like it, yet so different.

"This is cozy, ain't it, Andy? I always like to ride in the rain. When I was knee-high to a grasshopper, I used to go to town with my folks. We went in the family carriage and had two horses we called Kate and Bess. When it rained, we put on side-curtains, buckled them front and back. There was a curtain in front to protect those in the front seat. That curtain had an isinglass window in it, and the reins went out through a flap in front of the driver. Sometimes I'd ride up in front, but I liked it best when I was in the back seat, with my parents in front, so interested in talking to each other that they didn't notice me. I'd curl up under a robe and have all sorts of a good time by myself. Usually I'd go to sleep, for the sound of the rain on the curtains was a mighty soothin' thing, and the sloggin' of the horses' feet made a good accompaniment. The things man has made have changed, Andy, but God's things stay the same. I can remember Grandma Hester telling how she remembered the rain on the wagon-top on their trip west right after they were married. We don't travel in mud any more, but the patter of the rain is the same whether it's on a covered wagon or a station wagon."

"The moral to that is—?"

"That God Himself doesn't change. And Jesus Christ is the same yesterday, today, and forever. It's a privilege beyond compare to have given my son and my son's son to Him for His great harvest field. It compensates for the fact that I had to stay behind."

Andy winced again, then quickly took mental refuge in the assurance to himself that he still expected to serve his Master even though it was not to be in a distant land. There surely was a bit of work to be done in this country.

They turned off the highway onto a gravel road that led

between forest trees on either side. Grandpa looked around him with an air of satisfaction.

"Still here," he said happily. "Every time I come down I am anxious to see if Bill Putney has cut off this timber. It and my forty behind the wheatfield are the only virgin stands that are left in the county. I don't like to see it go, but time moves on and the greed of man needs more acres for wheat. Do you know son, that we are travelin' the old road that Thomas and Hester Lewis traveled one hundred twenty-five years ago? Henry and Sarah Putney were with them."

"Was it a road then?"

"Well, they got through. If I remember rightly what I've been told and what I read in Hester's old diary, the men had come the year before and hewed out the road and put up a couple of log houses. Then they went back and married the girls that had been waiting for them. This must have looked like the end of civilization to those girls. They came from Virginia, and that was a prosperous and cultured place even then. Sarah, especially, must have been shocked at what she had let herself in for. She came from a wealthy family and had a good education. To come down to a log cabin in the hills here was quite a step. This was brand-new country to the white men. There were a lot of settlements along the rivers, and had been ever since the days of George Rogers Clark. But nobody'd got back into these hills yet, and the Indians were as plentiful as the whites."

"It took real men and women to face that kind of life, didn't it? Our pioneer ancestors must have been a hardy tribe."

"No hardier than those of today. Life is different, but it still calls for a lot of gumption and backbone. Look what our boys are facing all over the world. I guess it didn't take any more courage to travel the wilderness trails in a covered wagon with Indians on every side than it takes now to fly a jet plane. The Lewises and the Putneys were no braver in facing the life of pioneers in a new land than their de-

72

scendants are in going into the African bush. No. Henry and Sarah and Thomas and Hester wouldn't need to be ashamed of you and Kay. You've got some gumption, too!"

Andy pressed his foot harder on the gas pedal and the car shot forward more rapidly. He wished he could think of some conversational topic that did not lead, in Grandpa's thinking, to missionary service. Not being able to do that, he resolved to bring this journey to an end as soon as possible. Coming out of the woods, they rounded a curve and saw the farm stretched before them, the original tract that Thomas Lewis had bought from the government.

"I always watch for the elm trees in the front yard," said Grandpa. "They were planted the day my father's baby brother was born. Father always called them Benjy's elms."

It was a beautiful picture even in the rain, the big "new house" that had been built when Grandpa's father was a toddler. Behind it was the old log cabin where Hester and Thomas had lived, and which she had refused to leave after he had gone. Beyond the houses stood the barns and sheds. Stretching away on each side were the orchards and garden and farther out, the fields of stubble or corn.

Other homes could be seen across the fields half-hidden behind their trees or standing out clearly on a hillside. On the highest hill, the one that stood out dimly now against the gray sky, the old white church lifted its steeple like a long finger pointing skyward. To Andy the whole beautiful, peaceful scene held a quality he had never noticed before. It seemed a symbol of the security and serenity for which his heart yearned. It spoke of labor with its reward of plentiful provision; of friends whose roots had sprung from the same soil and whose interests were the same. It was a place where one could live and labor and die, secure in the love of family and friends, with no mumbo-jumbo of black worship to haunt his dreams and break his heart by its devilish hold on the souls of poor creatures too weak and stupid to resist it. This place was where he belonged. It was home!

Chapter Ten

As the car turned into the yard, Sid came running from the house. "Gramps and Doc! You're a sight for sore eyes."

Unashamedly he kissed the old man, then turned to Andy and spoke huskily, "Doc, I hope you know we've been praying for you. It's tough to lose a dad at any time, but like this— just when you're ready—" His voice broke entirely and the tightening of his arm around Andy's shoulders had to convey the finish of the sentence.

He led them into the house apologizing for the cluttered condition of the kitchen.

"Grace and the kids left this morning. The Putney boys came over right away and we got busy. You can tell by the results that most of our work so far has been destructive rather than constructive. But we've really a system whether it shows or not. They left a few minutes ago, and I was just starting to do the chores. After that I'll rustle up some chow. Hope you're not too hungry."

"I've a better plan. While Grandpa rests a bit and you do the chores, I'll get supper. I'm a better cook than you are, Gunga Din!"

"Sez you! But you've got yourself a job, Sawbones. Help yourself to anything you can find in the pantry, cellar, or refrigerator. Grace left a lot of stuff cooked up. And there's a watermelon in a sack hanging down the old well. I intended to eat it all by myself, but I'll divide."

Sid went off to the barn, Grandpa lay down on the davenport, and Andy turned to his task of getting a meal. As he worked he seemed to see the big old kitchen peopled with folks he loved. Grandma was there, bustling about with a checked gingham apron tied about her waist, the starched strings in a big bow at the back. Mother was there, his mother, whose face he had almost lost in the mist of years. It came back clearly now with a smile that warmed his lonely heart. Dad was there, too, sitting by the table where Grandma was taking the fresh ginger cookies from the pans, taking a cookie or two from every pan as it came from the oven, and pulling Grandma's apron strings when she passed him; and Grandma, seeming to forget that he was not still a little boy who needed discipline, boxed his ears and scolded, "Behave yourself or I'll take you out to the shed!"

Andy laughed, as he sliced ham, at the idea of anyone boxing Dad's ears. Then he started at the strange sound of that laugh. It was the first time in three weeks that he had really laughed. Somehow this old kitchen, where the smell of ginger cookies and spiced apples seemed to linger, had taken him out of himself and set him back into another world and another day. He was not Dr. Andrew Lewis, disillusioned and heartsick. He was little Andy Lewis who had a laughing, blue-eyed Mother to tell him stories and to sing him funny little songs she made up as she went along, and a Dad who could romp and tease, discipline or pray as the occasion demanded. It was good to be here in the quiet of the country, and tonight at least he would relax and forget—forget that little overgrown burial plot in the Congo where one new grave slashed across the sod, forget the black man who had loved and been loved but had cast it all aside for the allurements of the Devil. He would even forget Kay, for until he knew what her answer to his letter would be, he must not let himself start to dream. He would just remember the days when life was good, and they were all together under this friendly old roof.

By the time Sid came in with the milk pails Grandpa was

75

ready to help get it strained into the cans and put into the cooler. Then they sat down to supper, and Andy's heart felt a balm as he heard Grandpa's voice asking God's blessing on the meal.

"That's the best meal I've eaten since my wife left me about ten hours ago," said Sid pushing back his chair. "Dr. Lewis, you've made yourself a job. You are elected head cook, second cook, and bottle-washer for the duration. Can do?"

"Can do, and will do, if it will help you at all. I don't have to be back until I get ready."

"Help me? Man, it will save my whole plan. If I don't have to quit and get dinner every day, we can finish this job in good shape. I lost three hours today on cooking and dish-washing. Boy, how those Putneys can eat! Now, if it weren't for the chores—"

"Don't you worry about the chores," said Grandpa. "I may be a bit less agile than I was fifty years ago, but I can still feed chickens and milk a dozen cows with that contraption of yours. Just you tend to your business, and I'll tend to the chores."

"That was what I hoped you would say. Maybe you'd best work together. If Doc needs help at noon, Gramps can give it. And then Doc can help get the feed for the cows, and take the milk into town. I'll just forget the farm work and go into the plumbing and heating business for a while."

"Where do we bunk tonight?"

"Well, Gramps' room is always ready, and you can have your pick of anything in the house except that and my bed. There's the two cribs in the kids' room, but you might not fit. Then there's a cot in the hall, and the davenport. On second thought I'd give up my bed for the sake of a good cook."

"I've a better thought. Is the old house still furnished?"

"Sure. Do you want to sleep there? It isn't wired for electricity, but I can run an extension cord from the shed. As far as I know it's just like it was the last time your folks

76

were home. All it needs would be some linens. Do you really want it?"

"Yes, if you don't mind."

"Go ahead, and use it," chimed in Grandpa. "It hasn't been changed a bit. We didn't need it for anything else, and I kinda liked to leave it the way Grandma Hester left it. All her things are in there."

"I've plenty of other beds," said Sid. "I was joking about putting you on the davenport. There's a perfectly good room upstairs. That old tick out there is stuffed with straw and the featherbed is hot as a griddle."

"I don't care. I want to sleep there. I'll probably roll out the trundle bed and sleep on it."

"You'll hang over the end."

"Two feet at least. But I've slept on worse. Let me have my way, Sid. I haven't been sleeping well, and out there I can tumble all I please and bother no one."

Out in the log cabin that had been Hester Lewis' home for nearly seventy years, the furnishings were just as she had left them. The largest room was combination kitchen, dining-room and living-room, with a great fireplace at one end. At the other end was the iron range that she had been persuaded to use in the later years of her life, but the fireplace had not been closed. There was still the big dropleaf table, the smaller work table, the homemade bookcases, the straight chairs, the long bench by the window, and the rockers with gingham cushions. On the mantel stood the Seth Thomas clock, the punched tin lantern, the candle molds that had been objects of wonder to little Andy Lewis on his visits to America.

In the bedroom was the huge chest of drawers, the bed where his parents had slept, and the trundle bed which had been his own. Here they had lived on their furloughs, eating their meals in the big house with Grandpa and Grandma, but coming here for the quiet times they needed as a family. It was strangely comforting to Dr. Andrew Lewis to come alone to this place and, for the first time since that cablegram came, to relax completely and not even think of the problems he must face.

Some day soon he would surely hear from Kay and learn her reaction to his decision. Perhaps she would despise him as a weakling, thinking he had been influenced in his decision by his love for her. But he believed that she would realize that he, as well as she, had to be honest, and would respect him for his courage. She had said she would always love him. She would surely see that God still meant them to be together. But until he knew what course she would take, he could not determine his own. Because he dared not face another disappointment, he would not let himself think of the possibilities. He must not let himself dream of what might be. For if it couldn't be, he didn't want to live through the crash of another dream. From now on he'd play it safe. But even while he argued thus, he was assuring himself that Kay would see it as he did. She would realize that he could not go out to Africa while his whole being revolted against it. He could make her understand that he was not thinking of her at all when he made his decision, and she would not condemn him. Some day soon, when she came back from her trip, he would see her and—Again he brought himself up sharply. He would *not* think of that.

Resolutely he settled himself to sleep in the great featherbed that seemed to engulf him in its depths. Perhaps it was as hot as Sid predicted it would be, but he did not care. From outside came the chirping of crickets and the soft rustle of night birds in the thicket behind the old house. At the foot of the hill he could hear the creek where the small waterfall splashed over its rocks and made a tune that was as soothing as a lullaby. For the first time in three weeks he sank into a sound sleep.

Chapter Eleven

WHEN HARRY AND RAY PUTNEY ARRIVED the next morning, they greeted Andy heartily but with noticeable self-consciousness, which might have been attributed to his father's death—or to the fact that until a few weeks ago they had expected him to marry their sister. He wondered, as they talked together, how much they knew of his and Kay's affairs, but no word gave him a clue. They did speak at last of his father's death, expressing their sympathy, but of Kay there was no word. And he did not ask. In time, the right time, he would hear from her. Until then he was just the cook on the "old Lewis farm."

He enjoyed the task of cooking and the feeling that he was being useful. He was very fond of Sid's wife and was eager to help in this project to surprise her. He offered his services in installing the plumbing, building kitchen cabinets, or laying linoleum. But Sid declined his aid.

"Not that I don't think you could do it, Doc," he said apologetically. "But we're falling over each other now with three of us on the job. Harry and Ray know this stuff, for they've just finished building Ray's new place, and they don't have to stop to figure it out. So no time's lost. Thanks, Doc, but if you'll just do the cooking and help Grandpa with the chores, you'll be worth your weight in uranium to us."

Andy accepted this with understanding, but the cooking and chores did not fill his time. Mornings were busy, for he helped Grandpa in the dairy and drove into town with the milk and

79

bought supplies. He canned some of the tomatoes that were wasting in the garden. Preparations for the noon meal took several hours, for his boarders had voracious appetites. He was thankful for the experience he had acquired at his mother's side in a Congo kitchen.

But these duties were over when the dinner dishes were washed and had been put back into the cupboards. There were at least three hours until time for evening chores and supper preparation. Grandpa went upstairs each day for his afternoon nap. Andy tried napping also, but found that he only grew more restless as he tossed on the hot bed or lay in the hammock under the trees. He tried reading, but he found his mind wandering from the printed page to a laughing face with merry blue eyes and a bridge of freckles across a turned-up nose. He did not want to think of that face now, so he gave up the reading and, instead, went for long walks in the woods.

The woods are not at their best in August. The fresh greenness of spring has gone and the flamboyance of autumn has not arrived. This year there had been scant rainfall, and the bushes were gray with dust. Somehow the whole scene seemed in harmony with his own outlook on life—the freshness gone and the beauty withered. He tried to keep his mind away from any definite analyzing or planning for the future. He looked for something else to fill his thoughts, and remembered how he and the three Putneys had once started a collection of leaves and flowers from these very woods. He wondered if some one of them might still have the book they had made with its specimens fastened down with adhesive tape. Maybe he would make another one now. It would be fun to compare the two. But the leaves were dried and dusty, and August is not a good month for flowers, so after a short time he gave it up. It was a childish project, no occupation for a man.

He followed the dried-up rocky bed of the little brook on another day, and after some climbing that left him out of breath, found himself on a broad flat rock. He remembered that in seasons when the usual amount of rain fell, a stream of water flowed from the crevice in the rock and tumbled down the hill to join the creek. Now this, too, was dry and dusty. It reminded him of his own life. The springs that had seemed fresh and never-failing a few months ago had now dried completely. All the joy of his life had left him with the abandonment of his plan to go to Africa. He missed that plan and dream, yet it was abhorrent to him. Had he not known Africa, had its customs and life been as yet an unsolved mystery to him, he might have gone. He might have in his ignorance seen it through a sheen of glamor. But he knew it too well to be tempted by it.

No, he did not have any regrets for Africa. But he had no other plans or purpose to take the place of the former ones. He supposed, of course, that he would find a place to practice, but just now he had no heart for the starting of any career. There had come an offer from a hospital in a distant state where a young surgeon was needed as assistant to an older surgeon whose name was famous in medical circles. He had refused it, but maybe it was still open. He didn't really care. Something would develop when he was ready for it. Just now he did not feel competent to do so much as remove a splinter!

He climbed onto the top of the rock and looked out over the valley. Far below him lay the house he had left an hour ago. Farther off he could see the stately home of the Putneys. Like a white ribbon across the valley and through the gap between the hills stretched the road—the road that had been only a wilderness trail when the first Putneys and Lewises had followed it a century and a quarter ago. Since then five other generations of Putneys and Lewises had lived and labored in the valley, and had left their mark on the community and the state. That was a way of life that paid! Surely that was the way God meant men to live, in pleasant homes among friends and neighbors, with mutual love, productive toil, and no weird noises and repulsive sights of heathenism to turn the soul sick.

On a hill across the valley he could see the big tree where he and Kay had sat while she told him the story of the first Kate Putney and Andrew Lewis, a story to have so soon its counterpart in their own lives. At the memory of that other unhappy love story, his heart grew heavy. Was his and Kay's love to suffer the same fate, or would she receive him back with his broken plans? What did lie ahead for him? Would he be able to find a place like that little white and green village he could see beyond the crossroads, where he could work and serve and be happy like other men, or would he always feel as listless and indifferent to life as he did now?

As he started down the hill again he thought with wry amusement, "Eight years of costly training, and I'm working as a cook on a farm! It would be a good joke if there were anyone here to appreciate it."

On Sunday they went to church in the old frame building where Thomas and Hester Lewis had worshiped. It had recently been remodeled, and an educational building built in the back. But the old part, with its stiff, straight pews, its plain glass windows, and its square bell tower was left as it had always been. The new coat of paint seemed to give it renewed youth, and the work of those pioneer hands gave promise of many years of service to come. Grandpa sat proudly between his grandsons and listened with happy concentration to a sermon that was trite and uninspiring to Andy. Sid seemed to find it sufficient, also, and Andy wondered if they really enjoyed it, or if they just accepted it from habit. When on the way home they expressed their favorable opinions of it, he listened in silence, offering no comment. If that was what they liked, let them like it!

After dinner they all drove "up the creek" to a small country church where Sid and Grace helped in the Sunday school. Andy would have preferred to stay at home, but Grandpa was so eager for him to see the little church that he could not deny him. As they drove along in Sid's small truck up the twisting gravel road that led to the out-of-the-way community, Grandpa chattered happily about it.

"Hester and Thomas Lewis started this church before the Civil War. And I guess there hasn't been a time since when some of the Lewises haven't been helpin' them."

"What's the matter with them that they still need help? A church that old should be able to go it alone, I'd think."

Sid kept still and let Grandpa do the talking. "Yes, I know that's the way it seems. But you see, it's a mighty poor little place. The land up there is so poor that it won't even grow weeds! I've often wondered myself why anybody keeps livin' there. But to those folks it is home same as the farm is to me. The people don't have time to study or read. Some of the young folks go to school and learn better ways of livin', but when they do that they don't make their homes here. So it still leaves the poorer, more ignorant ones to hold the farms. They'll always need help."

"Sounds hopeless to me. Does it pay to keep working there year after year with no results?"

"Oh, I didn't say we didn't have results. Sid here can tell you some stories that will make your eyes shine. He and Gracie are mighty proud of their boys and girls up here. Your Grandma and I came up here every Sunday afternoon as long as she lived, and I think it was because I heard Sid teach a class up here one day when he was visitin' us that made me willin' to let him have the farm. He's a grand teacher for boys!"

Sid laughed in embarrassment. "He's prejudiced, Doc. I really am a pretty poor teacher. If I had to teach in our own Sunday school I'd start to stuttering again and make a mess of it. But I love my hill boys and they love me and we get along."

"You bet you do!" said Grandpa proudly. "I sometimes wish Grandma Hester could see my fine boys. It would really make her eyes shine. And I wish you could have seen *her*. When she was all enthused over something, her big dark eyes would shine like stars, 'specially when it was something like

this she was enthused about. She really had a one-track mind."

"I thought from what I have heard of her that she had a very vigorous mentality and made herself felt all over the county!"

"Oh, she did, she surely did! But it was all a part of that one track. Grandma Hester had just one purpose in life. If she was here now, she'd be singin' the song Charlie's Jean sang in church a couple of weeks ago. It goes something like this,

> "Oh, to be saved from self, dear Lord,
> Oh, to be lost in Thee!
> Oh, that it might be no more I,
> But Christ that lives in me!

That was Grandma Hester all over. Some place back in her life before I came into it, she just let loose of self and let Christ take over. *That* was her one track."

After a few minutes of silence Andy asked, "Who does the preaching out here? Sid?"

"Not on your life." Sid laughed. "I'm a farmer. Our church pays a student from the seminary in Chilton to come out every other Sunday. He won't be here today, so there will be only Sunday school. And by the way, Doc, Grace asked me to get a substitute for her class. In the rush of this week I forgot it. So—you're appointed."

"Me? A class of girls? You're crazy!"

"Nope. I think it would be a happy solution to my troubles. Here's the teacher's book. You can't let me down."

"Oh, can't I? Now if it were boys—"

"Ah, I've trapped you! You can have my boys and I'll take Grace's girls."

There being no way out, Andy had to agree. To complete his discomfort, Grandpa decided to attend the boys' class that day, and sat there with such a look of beatific satisfaction on his face that Andy found himself praying silently, "Oh, Lord, help me not to let him down!"

After he started talking to the boys he had no difficulty.

All during his college years he had gone every Sunday with a group of students to a small Sunday school in the poorer district of the nearby city and taught boys of this age. He knew that in spite of the differences of circumstance, boys are much the same the world over. Their hopes, desires, and needs are the same whether they are in the slums of a big city or in the poverty-stricken community "up the creek." So, laying aside the quarterly which he had not had time to study, he took the Bible that Grandpa handed him and started to talk as he had done to his city boys.

He told them of a young man named Saul who met Jesus one day as he traveled the Damascus road, and who from that time was so different that God changed his name. He told how this young man, who could have held a prominent place among the leaders of his people, became poor and sick and, eventually, a prisoner for the sake of his Lord. The boys sat entranced as the teacher, forgetting himself for the first time in many weeks, spoke of the work that Paul did as he went from country to country telling men of the One who had come to ransom them from sin. He told of the price paid in loneliness, in hunger, in mistreatment, even in misunderstanding by his friends. Then his voice softened as he spoke of Another, the One whom Paul loved, and showed Him in such winning sweetness that Paul was forgotten and his Master stood revealed to these boys as their own if they would have Him.

"I like to think that He can take us, even though we don't seem to have much that He could use, and bless our service just as He blessed Paul's. But first we must meet Him and own Him as Saviour, then we must call Him 'Master.' Sid told me that every boy in this class is a Christian. That is wonderful and shows you have had a teacher that knows how to lead boys to his Lord."

A chorus of, "You bet we have!" interrupted him and caused the members of other classes to turn and look questioningly in their direction.

Andy went on with a smile, "He's a great guy! I'm proud

to be his cousin. Now I'm wondering how many of you have taken the next step, that of letting Him be your Master. I'm not going to ask you to tell me. I see the superintendent getting ready to dismiss us. But let's all go home and talk it over with Him. Shall we? Grandpa, will you pray?"

The ride home was a silent one. Grandpa was tired, Sid seemed engrossed in his own thoughts, and Andy had no desire to disturb him. He had a letdown feeling as if he had been carried out of himself and gone farther than he realized, farther than he had thought he could. He remembered once when he was about sixteen, he and David had been coming back from a trip to a village and David, falling on a loose rock as they went down a steep hillside, had broken his leg. Andy hadn't dared leave him while he went for help, so without considering whether he *could* do it or not, he had carried David home across his shoulders. It had only been a bit over a mile, but everyone on the station had been astounded that he could do it. He had tried later to lift someone of that weight and could not do it. The need of the moment had taken him out of himself and given him other strength. He remembered now how weak he had felt afterward. He had that same almost overwhelming weakness now. He wanted to get into his room and relax completely.

Grandpa, however, had other ideas. In spite of his weariness he wanted to go to the cemetery up by the church.

"I haven't been up there since I came home," he explained. "I always like to go up there on a sunny Sunday afternoon. It does something for me."

"I know, Gramps," said Sid. "I'd like to take you, but I'm expecting a call from Grace. I'll let Doc do it."

Visiting a cemetery was the last thing that Andy desired to do, but for this dear old man who loved him he would do anything. The sun was low in the West, and the church with its quiet yard basked in the peculiar stillness of such a time and place. Grandpa moved reverently from one grave to another, touching the stones lovingly as he rambled on about the ones who slept beneath them. He seemed to hardly realize that Andy was there. At times he seemed to be speaking to the quiet sleepers.

"This is Mother's grave here. She's been gone four years now, and it's such a long time! I'll be comin' along soon, Bessie. I wish you could have seen our boys today. Maybe you did, I don't know. Here's my father and mother side by side. He's the only one of old Andrew's children that's here. My Uncle Benjy was buried out in Dakota where he was killed. And Aunt Mary died in India. It's comfortin' to know that when the Lord calls they will all come forth together no matter where their bodies lie now.

"This is Grandma Hester here. You were glad to lie down weren't you, Grandma? She was so tired at the last, and she had said good-bye to Thomas so many years before. And all these little ones had gone ahead fifty years or more before. Even Andrew—so long ago. It was a long, hard road you traveled, Grandma, no wonder you were tired."

He was quiet as he stooped to pull some weeds that had encroached on the lot.

"Don't you think we'd better go home?" Andy said gently. "You are tired, I know, and this doesn't rest you."

The old man went back to the car with no remonstrance, but as they drove down the hill he said quietly, "You're mistaken, boy. It does rest me. When I get up here, the things that fret and burden me all fade away. I am reminded, as I need to be ever so often, that all this is passing, and that all that matters is that we live so that the Lord won't be ashamed of us when He comes. After I've been up here, I can go home and not feel lonely any more. The strings that hold me to earth seem to be loosened, and the ones that draw me to heaven are tightening. There are more of my folks over there than are left here, and sometimes I get mighty homesick. But after I've been up there, I go home willin' to wait quietly."

Chapter Twelve

WHETHER GRANDPA WOULD AD-
MIT IT or not, he was so tired that he went to bed immediately
after supper. Sid drove off to attend the evening service in the
church. Andy refused his invitation to accompany him and
went out to the cabin to face a long evening. There were not
even any letters to write. To whom would he write now? For
years he had written a long letter to his father each week.
Occasionally he had written to David. Now there was no one.
If only he would hear from Kay, if only she would tell him
that she understood and that she believed, as he did, that God
meant them to live and serve Him in America.

He browsed through the books that were in the old hand-
made bookcases on each side of the fireplace. Probably all
the books that Thomas and Hester Lewis had ever owned were
here, a record of the literature and customs from those first
pioneer days in the wilderness, down to the time of Hester's
death more than seventy-five years later. There were the old
textbooks that Thomas had used in William and Mary College,
some law books that had apparently served as guides in the
community government of that long-ago settlement, one or
two devotional books, *Foxe's Book of Martyrs,* two very old
hymnals besides many of later date, and books of fiction,
some in paper covers, some in cloth now stained and
ragged. There were textbooks that had been used by Hester
Lewis' children, grandchildren, and great-grandchildren. The
illustrations in the old readers interested him for an hour—

the boys with round hats, short jackets, and trousers that ended halfway between the knee and ankle; the girls in long dresses and pantalets, with high shoes buttoned over striped stockings; babies with much-befrilled dresses that were long enough to reach the floor from the lap of a fond parent, men in long-tailed coats, high hats, and very fancy vests, and women with incredibly small waists and prim expressionless faces.

"Wow! And folks squawk about today's styles. Give me the bobby sox any day! And didn't the kids know how to do *anything* but roll hoops in those days?"

Going farther he found something else that fascinated him so completely that everything else was forgotten—the medical library of Hester Lewis. It consisted of three books, all designed to teach the pioneer of those early days and the house-keeper of the latter part of the century how to safeguard the family health. The first had been published in 1815 and probably had traveled over the mountains in the covered wagon on that long-ago wedding trip. The next was published forty years later and was inscribed, "To Mother from Andrew in the hope that she will find in its pages a new and more palatable kind of physick." The newest of them was a very fancy volume and had evidently been a Christmas gift. On its flyleaf was written in a flourishing script, "To Grandma, from Tom and Nellie and the children. If you are determined to dose us, here are the latest ideas on how to do it with the least pain to your patients. Dec. 25, 1882." Andy chuckled. Apparently Great-great-great-grandmother had been a self-made practitioner, and the family did not always enjoy her ministrations.

Long into the night he sat reading the old volumes, smiling over the scientific wisdom and ignorant superstition that were mingled together on the yellowed pages of the earlier books. He found directions for compounding remedies of plants that he knew to be the basis of many of the drugs that were in use even at the present day. He read solemn recommendations for tying a yarn string around the toe for "cow-itch," or binding a woolen sock that had been worn for several weeks around the neck in case of sore throat. There were explicit directions for bleeding a patient. This seemed to be standard procedure for almost every ailment.

"And today we give them blood," he murmured.

He read that to hide a few hairs of the patient in a hollow tree would effect a cure if the moon were just right. And his nose wrinkled in horror as he learned of the many uses for skunk oil. There were directions for many kinds of poultices— bread and milk, freshly killed meat, onions fried and applied hot, and peach leaves pounded to a pulp. At the side of this latter, faded writing stated that "this one works." Apparently Grandma Hester could not recommend all of them.

"And yet folks kept on living, in spite of their remedies," Andy mused. "They lived and were able to endure hardship and toil that we could not stand up to at all. From what I hear Hester Lewis rode all over these hills, or climbed afoot when the roads were too steep for the old horse and cart. She probably saved more lives than I ever will. Even now folks rise up and call her blessed."

These books proved to be a blessing, for on the nights when he could not sleep (and these were becoming all too many), he could turn on his light without fear of annoying anyone, and read until the crowing of the roosters and the restlessness of the barnyard animals told of another day—a day to be lived through, but not to be filled with any of the zest of life that made days enjoyable.

After a week the monotony of the work he was doing began to wear on his nerves, and he became increasingly despondent. He began to dislike being around Grandpa because of the old man's constant references to the supposed approaching departure. Each such reference was bitterness to his soul. He knew he should face the task of telling both Grandpa and the Board of his defection from the course to which he had declared himself dedicated. He knew it would have to be done sometime, for *never* would he go to the Congo or any other mission field.

He had a feeling of self-loathing when he realized how many years had been spent in his training, and how those years had been paid for by the sacrifices not only of his father and grandfather, but of many other people who had expected to have a share through him in sending out the Gospel. He felt that he had cheated them, and he vowed that if God would grant him sufficient success in his career here, he would pay the way of some other young doctor who could go out in his stead—some fellow who had not already paid an overwhelming price for the salvation of the Congo.

But he could feel no regret at his decision. Rather, he began to feel resentful to those to whom he felt he owed this obligation. What right had they to shackle him in this way? Even the memory of his father lost its sweetness. Had he not unduly influenced an impressionable child to carry out dreams of his own? And the son, loving the father passionately, had imagined that God wanted him to take up the work the father must, inevitably, lay down.

Night after night he tossed restlessly or rose to read through the long hours or to walk down the lane and sit by the creek trying to get from the night a quietness of spirit that would enable him to sleep. He vowed that never again would he feel a sense of impatience with those querulous patients who complained of sleepless hours. He had always secretly considered sleeplessness a weakness that could be overcome by a bit of will power. Now, he knew it for what it was, a torturing agony that left body and mind exhausted.

On other nights he would forget his good intentions and would allow himself to think of Kay. Could he ever convince her that he had been entirely objective in coming to his decision, or would she believe he was doing it because of her, and despise him for it? At times she would seem very real and close to him. He would waken from a dream with her voice in his ears and the sight of her laughing face before him. He would reach out to touch her, only to find her gone. Then the memory of the thing that had separated them would return to him, and he would be sure that she could never understand nor accept his action.

In the morning he would try to convince himself that now the barrier between them was gone and they could find a fruition of their love in a life of service here at home. Surely they could be married now. She had said she would always love him, and of course he still loved her. He loved her so much that he was sick with longing for her.

But when he tried to plan for that future together, the joy of it was gone, and he grew despondent again. The dreams would not return. Perhaps it was because she was not with him to help him in those daydreams. When she came back, together they would build the air castles again. Until then he could only draw back from even that picture in distaste. Oh, if only she would write!

Chapter Thirteen

IT WAS A RAINY EVENING that carried with it a chill that made the air seem more like that of October than late August. They had had an early supper and Grandpa had gone to bed. Sid was working alone, laying the new linoleum tiles in the kitchen and declined any help.

"Please, Doc, I want to do as much of this myself as I can. I don't want you guys in on my wife's birthday present any more than is necessary."

So Andy had retired alone to the cabin. He had thrown some paper and wood into the fireplace and lighted a fire to remove the clammy chill. Restless and unsatisfied he turned to the old bookcases for entertainment. From the top shelf he took a gray old ledger, thinking to amuse himself for an hour or so with the farm and household accounts of Thomas and Hester Lewis. The book was not an account book however. It was designated in the front as "The Diary of Hester Evaline Lewis," and underneath the title was an explanatory paragraph written in the painstaking script of a schoolgirl.

I am Hester Lewis. I was married to Thomas Lewis yesterday, and tomorroy we will start west with Sarah and Henry Putney. It will be my first jurney and I want a rekurd of it. Thomas bot me this book. I will rite in it ever day.

She had not literally kept her promise to write every day, but through almost eighty years she had treasured this book, and in it kept a record of her life and her thoughts and of the lives of those whose course touched her own. Sometimes she did write every day for weeks. Then in days of busyness or stress or in times of smooth-going monotony she had let months go by without writing at all. Invariably the need to express herself would drive her back to her ledger, and the story would go on.

Andy Lewis did not expect to read the diary. Diaries had never interested him. He had always thought they were a pastime for foolish girls or weak-minded men. He did think to read a page or two of this just out of curiosity. Strange that a person could have been dead more than fifty years and this paper, so unsubstantial, so easily destroyed, should have survived to hold the thoughts and yearnings of that soul. He sat down in the old Morris chair that still held the hollows made by Hester Lewis' body and began to read her diary. Through that evening and long into the night he read, and for other evenings until he had finished it, forgetting his own heartaches and longings, oblivious of the rain that beat on the roof, or the moonlight that shone the next night. He lost all sense of time and place and was back with the sixteen-year-old Hester and her twenty-one-year-old husband as they crossed the mountains and forded the rivers and fought their way through the swamps to reach this place where they had planned their first home.

He read it with a sense of reverent awe. All that was mortal of Hester and Thomas Lewis had been returned to the earth long before he, Andrew Lewis, was born. Their spirits were with the God that gave them. But the record was still here and, although he did not know it then, the reading of that story marked the greatest crisis in his life. Having read it he could never be the same.

94

BOOK II
INTERLUDE

Chapter Fourteen

IT WAS IN THE EARLY FALL of 1821 that two heavily laden wagons creaked along over the rough trail that led toward the rolling hills of the southern Illinois country, where Henry Putney and Thomas Lewis had bought land from the government. It seemed to Hester that they had been on the road more weeks than she could count. All the years in the cabin on the Clinch River in western Virginia seemed strange and far away from her.

The girl who had lived and worked and dreamed through those years was a complete stranger to the woman who now rode a bony roan horse behind the ox-drawn wagon or walked beside her husband as he strode ahead of the slow-moving animals. In those weeks they had climbed hills, forded streams, wound through tortuous mountain trails, evaded Indians, and struggled through forest roads that still held stumps and roots which threatened to overturn the wagons. Twice because of heavy rains they had been obliged to camp for days alongside a river to wait until the stream became low enough for them to ford. When each day had become so dark that they could no longer see the trail, they had camped where they were and slept in their wagons. As these wagons were piled high with household furnishings, farming equipment, clothing, and the food staples that would keep them until the next year's crops came, the sleeping was far from comfortable, but they dared not sleep on the ground. They had cooked their meals over a fire which they built in the trail lest it spread into the woods around them. Each night they prepared enough food for the following day so that the stops for meals and to feed the animals might be as short as possible.

They had been impatient with the slow-moving oxen, but horses could never have stood the rigors of the trail with the weight of the wagons to burden them. So day after day they plodded along. The mountains had given place to hills, and these in turn to broad stretches of grass-covered plains where settlers' homes were beginning to have a look of comfort and permanence. Here Hester and Sarah would have liked to stop the weary trek and settle down. But the men shook their heads.

"This Kentucky country is too old for us. The land is already sky-high in this blue grass. It will be the richest place in the West some day. We can't afford it even if we could get it. The land farther up in Illinois is going pretty high, too. Along the Illinois and Sangamon it costs so much to buy a farm that we would not be able to get a toe hold," explained Thomas, and Henry joined in, telling of the advantages of their own choice.

"We spent weeks out here looking around and we think we have the best bargain west of the mountains. It is a valley between two ranges of low but rocky hills. Some folks say they are the foothills of the Ozarks off west of the Mississippi, but I don't know. That seems a long way for even a mountain's feet to reach! There haven't been many settlements out there because it's not near any river. But there's a fine creek running through the valley and we have figured that by deepening several shallows we can float our rafts over to the Skillet Fork, then to the Little Wabash, and on down to the Wabash. Oh, we've got it all figured out, haven't we, Thomas?"

"At least we *think* we have," admitted Thomas. "In a few years the roads will be better and wagons will get in to build up a trade. I believe that before long we will be able to haul our grain to market and drive the stock overland. It's a coming country, we are sure."

"Is ours as pretty as this?" questioned Hester, looking out over the rolling Kentucky fields." "I never seed suchlike before."

"I never *saw*, honey," corrected Thomas gently.

She obediently said, "I never *saw* suchlike before," then burst out irrepressibly, "Well, I don't care, nohow! I done hear'd — I mean I heard — that the Illinois country is the best ever. That's what we'll have, I'm shore!"

And for the fortieth time he told her, as he strode along by the oxen's heads and she walked beside him to rest her weary limbs, "It's a beautiful spot, my Hettie. In the valley we can raise any kind of crops. The slopes will make good pasture lands and orchards, and the hills and woods will protect them from the severe cold. There is wood enough for all the logs and fuel we need, and there's a brook tumbling down from the hillside that will give us plenty of clear, cold water. I think it's perfect, sweet."

Henry had gone back to ride in the wagon with Sarah and the two were alone. Hester asked anxiously, "Is Henry's land so good, too? 'Twould be a pure pity if we had all the good."

"You blessed angel! Henry thinks his is better. He had more money than I, and he bought over five hundred acres of the valley land. We had to pay two dollars an acre for the valley, and I got my woods and hills for just half of that. I didn't want all lowland anyway."

"I wouldn't want a farm withouten ary woods."

" 'Without *any* woods,' Hettie. Neither would I. We have enough flat land to raise good crops, all I can tend to until I get me some big sons to help. I don't know what Henry will do with so much land. He will have to hire a lot of help. Our woods and hills will serve a mighty useful purpose. And we've a stout house that will keep us warm and comfortable until we can build more. I hope you'll be happy there, my Hettie."

"Oh, I will! I air—I mean I am—so happy just bein' with you that I crave to sing!"

"Why don't you sing, then? Sing the Doxology. We're coming to the Ohio, and that's the last big river to cross!"

So while they waited on the bank for the huge log raft that would ferry them across the river, Hester sang. Sarah heard it back in the wagon where she had been sobbing in homesick loneliness, and she was comforted and given strength to face the hard way that lay ahead and which she had felt was too much for her. Henry Putney heard it and noting its effect on Sarah, was glad for Hester's strong, true voice and courageous heart. The two ferrymen heard it and were awed at the tune they had forgotten in the rigors of this wild country. And Thomas Lewis lifted up his heart in thanksgiving to God for the gift of a woman whose love and faith would light his way in this wilderness. Each of them thanked her for the song, and she wrote in her diary by the campfire that night her own thanks for being able to "pleasure" so many hearts.

After they crossed the Ohio, they turned from the more traveled road into the rutted one that led into the hill country. Often they had to stop while Henry and Thomas cut off low-hanging branches that would have damaged the canvas top of the wagons, or chopped and dragged away some tree that had fallen across the road since the last wagon came through. Sixty years later Hester Lewis went back to Virginia to visit. She made the trip in less than two days, in a railway coach with green velvet upholstery, hanging kerosene lamps, and a stove that kept the car, even in winter, so warm she could *almost* have been comfortable without her coat. Sixty years after that another Lewis made the entire distance in twelve hours, streaming along the concrete highway and declaring he hadn't really hurried! But in 1821 the wagons sometimes did not make five miles a day. And on some days they could not travel at all. So, although the August sun had been hot when they left Virginia, an early snow lay on the ground when they halted on the top of the last hill, and looked down upon the valley that lay before them.

They stood there together, four young people hardly past childhood, facing an unknown future. Off to the left they could see Henry Putney's cabin built under two great oaks that would keep off the summer sun and facing the lowland meadows where Henry could begin plowing in the spring without the labor of clearing timber from his land. To the right lay the acres that Thomas Lewis had purchased. There was a goodly stretch of lowland which was now covered with the ripe corn that was awaiting husking. There was a high, clean meadow where next year's grain could be grown, and woods that would furnish the fuel for the cold weather that lay ahead of them. The cabin was hardly discernible through the trees, and Hester, as she looked at it, felt a thrill of tenderness at the sight.

"Hit war just like a chicken tucked under a hen's wing," she wrote. "I knowed hit war mine and hit would everly be mine. I loved it so much I got the all-overs when I looked at hit!"

Dr. Andrew Lewis, lying in his bed in Hester's cabin more than a century and a quarter later, listened to the rain on the roof and thought, "She is gone, and yet this place 'everly' belongs to her!"

Chapter Fifteen

Housekeeping in the cabin was little more than play to the strong, young girl who, ever since she could remember, had worked for her keep in a house where she was at the beck and call of a busy and fretful woman. From the hour when she had arisen in the darkness until she had been allowed to go to bed after all the family had retired, she had known nothing but labor. Life as an orphaned "hired girl" had not been easy, and freedom from the dominance of a scolding mistress was almost more than she could comprehend. She felt a fresh joy every day in the possession of her own home. She who had had only a third of a trundle bed each night, and no place to keep even a pretty ribbon she might have acquired, now had an entire house to call her own.

And, more than all other joys combined, she had the love of the most "grand and fine" man on earth. She could not forget the marvel of that. Sometimes when she sat alone by the fire hemming sheets from the bolt of cotton that Thomas' mother had given, or when she lay by his side on the featherbed that kept them warm on the cold nights, she thought back over it all, and it seemed like a story—the kind of a story that might be written in a picture book someone would give to a child for a lovely present, but a story that could never, never happen to anyone.

She remembered that day many months ago when two young men had stopped at the Kearney home and asked for help. One of them, Henry Putney, had cut his foot with his ax, and the wound needed attention. They had been allowed to sleep in the loft of the barn, and Mrs. Kearney provided hot water and old cloths for dressing the cut. Hester, seeing that it was badly inflamed, ventured the information that a peach leaf poultice would help, and had gathered the leaves, pounded them to a pulp and helped to apply them. For three weeks the young men waited there, and when they were ready to go on to the West where they would homestead some of the land the government was selling, Thomas Lewis had won Hester's promise that when he came east again she would go back with him.

During the time of waiting, while she had tried to acquire with her meager wages the clothing and linens a bride would need, she could hardly convince herself that she was not dreaming. Yet here she was. The house was real, the farm was real, and most real and wonderful of all was Thomas Lewis with his kind, sweet smile and his never-failing devotion to her. She would wonder at it all, and thrill at it, and go to sleep with Thomas' arm around her.

It was on one such night when the snow lay in deep drifts around the cabin and the wind blew until the great trees outside groaned and bent before it, that Hester was awakened by a pounding on the door. In affright she cried out to Thomas, and together they hastened to open the heavy panel. Two snow-covered figures staggered in, one to fall in a heap on the floor. By the time Thomas and Hester had forced the door shut against the wind, Sarah was crying in exhaustion, and Henry was brushing the snow from her face and hair.

"Our house burned!" he gasped. "We couldn't do a thing to save it. It's gone!"

"Oh! cried Hester. "Sarah, you air shakin' all over. You're purely froze. You shuck off them clothes and get into some of mine. I'll tuck you right into my bed."

Over Sarah's remonstrances she was put to bed, while Thomas stirred up the fire and put the kettle on. With a cup of hot tea in his hands Henry, between the sips which were bringing warmth back into his body, told the story.

"Caesar wakened me by barking, and I found the flames eating into the logs beside the chimney. If the wind hadn't been so strong, I might have saved it. But it was no use to even try. We got our heavy wraps on and saved all we could. We got out her chest and our clothes and the chairs we brought from back home. We piled the dishes and pans in the tubs and carried them out. I got my books and the feather-bed and the blankets, but when I started back after more of the furniture, the roof was falling, and I didn't dare. We put the clothes and the chest and the bedding and books in the hay shed. The other things are sitting out in the snow. Then we came over here. The wind is pretty strong. Sarah's about worn out."

"She shorely is, but don't you fret none. We got that shuck tick Henry slept on last year. You and Thomas can sleep on it on the floor and Sarah and me will take the bed."

In the morning Thomas and Henry hitched the oxen to the big homemade sled and drove down the road to where only a few charred chunks of wood and a tall stone chimney were left of the Putney cabin. They brought back all of the things that had been saved. Even the oxen, the cow, the dozen hens, and two pigs were brought to share the quarters of the Lewis' livestock. For the rest of that winter the two families lived together while Thomas and Henry labored to build another house. The loft, where Hester hoped some day to tuck in her own boys and girls, was hastily converted into another bedroom. Here Sarah and Henry stored the things they had saved, and here, as the winter passed, Henry added to the store new chairs, a table, and a bed to replace the ones that had been burned. Whenever the weather was too bad for them to work out-of-doors, the men sawed and planed and hammered, and one by one the new pieces grew under their hands. By spring Sarah would have her house furnished again.

In her diary Hester confessed that though she felt bad

about the loss her friends had suffered, she could not but be glad that the two families were under one roof during that first hard winter. For the snow piled high even in the woodlands. The path that the men had broken between the cabins became buried so deeply that the girls could not have traveled it. And had each been alone life would have become hard indeed, especially for Sarah who had left a lovely home and a devoted family behind, and who was not adjusting easily to frontier life. Hester, having known hardship in her former life, did not feel the lack of comforts now. She sang and worked through the days, and after Henry and Sarah had climbed to their loft at night and Thomas had fallen asleep, she would creep from her bed and by the light of a candle placed in the shadow of the table so that it might not disturb Thomas, she would sit on the floor and write in her diary.

The men were kept very busy. The trip back from Virginia had consumed more time than expected, and the corn that should have been gathered in the fall now must be cut and husked in the winter. There was the cabin to be built, the furniture to be made, and always fuel to cut. Sometimes the girls would go to the field on the sled and try to help. Hester's strong hands were almost as efficient as the men's, but Sarah found it difficult. They would carry the husked corn into the cabin and shell it for the chickens, or grind it into meal for their own use. They had brought back several precious bags of wheat flour from the East, but it must be carefully meted out to last until more could be procured.

In the house there were things that Sarah could do that were beyond the clumsy efforts of Hester's workworn fingers.

"Let's teach each other!" Sarah suggested one day. She had wept because the men laughed at her bread. "I'll teach you how to make lace, and you show me how to bake bread that won't make even the pigs sick."

Hester agreed and the lessons began. The girls found that they could exchange other knowledge also. Sarah could knit and Hester could weave. One day when Thomas longed for a

105

feed basket, Hester came to the rescue. She showed him how to make flat strips with his drawknife from an ash sapling, and with these weave just the basket he needed. Then, as a reward, he wove her a clothesbasket. She brought from her trunk a piece of thin metal with a succession of holes in it, decreasing very gradually from over one-half inch in diameter to about one-sixteenth of an inch. An ash strip would be drawn through the largest hole then the next, each time losing a small portion of its fibers. By the time it had been drawn through the last hole they had a long, tough strand that could, when soaked in water, be woven into all sorts of fancy designs. It took the strong arms of the men to draw the strands through the metal, but even Sarah could weave the fancy baskets, and she proved to be very apt and clever at it. Under Hester's tutelage, she worked until she was sure of herself, then produced, in an original pattern of her own, a basket that was an exquisite bit of workmanship.

[That basket, darkened by time but with no break in the symmetrical scallops that formed its edge, went to the city with Sarah Putney's great-great-granddaughter, Kay Putney. Dr. Andrew Lewis remembered seeing it on her table in the apartment near Brainard Hospital.]

It was in the evening, however, that life in the cabin grew most interesting to Hester. She who had read only through the third book in the tattered readers in the little schoolhouse back on the Clinch River, sat in wonder as she listened to the discussions between the two men, both graduates of William and Mary College, and Sarah, who had had two years at a young ladies' Academy. She saw opened up to her a new world, one that she had not known to have existed. Except for the college textbooks that the men had brought with them, there were few books in the two families, but these few were thoroughly read and commented on during those evenings. There was a volume of American history, a book of orations that the men loved to read, rolling the phrases on their tongues in sonorous tones that were an imitation of the manner of their professor in college. And there were two books of poetry whose contents became one of Hester Lewis' lifelong joys.

But more than anything else the Bible drew and held her. She had never owned one. Indeed, there had not been one in the home in which she had been reared. She sat spellbound as Thomas and Henry read from it each evening before they retired. To her it was the audible voice of God, clear and unmistakable. Until her eyes closed in sleep she would meditate on what she had heard, and the next day as she sat hemming sheets or working on the appliquéd quilt she had started, she would become lost in abstraction, until Sarah impatiently would arouse her to conversation again.

She was so eager to learn more of the Book that she would, whenever possible, study it for herself, and when Thomas came in after the chores were done, she had a long list of words for his pronunciation and definition. So many questions about the meaning and truths of the Word came to her active mind that the others found themselves driven back again and again to its pages for the answers. Gradually the time spent on the Book grew longer each evening as its wonders unfolded through the real study they were driven into by the questions of the spiritually hungry girl. The Seth Thomas clock on the shelf—the only wedding present Hester had received—would often strike midnight before they brought the discussions to a close.

[Dr. Andrew Lewis lay in bed and listened to that same clock, and wondered what it would be like to hear the Bible for the first time, not to have had a background of family worship where the words of the Book were read and discussed until they became a part of one's very life. Would they mean more if they were newer? Would they have more power to transform, to comfort, to guide?]

Chapter Sixteen

IN FEBRUARY A BLIZZARD CAME. It was a storm that was to be talked of for many years. The snow piled deeper and deeper on the roads, blowing into hard-packed drifts that a man could walk on, but which broke under the weight of the oxen and made it impossible to use them. Thomas and Henry had to abandon the work on the cabin. The logs they had cut lay buried under many feet of snow. Even the site of the cabin became only a white hillock. At the Lewis cabin the woods formed somewhat of a windbreak, but even there the drifts reached the windows. When the clouds parted and the sun shone again, the temperature became colder, and for several weeks there was no hope of a thaw. The four young people had to think in terms of survival for themselves and the animals in the stables. It was impossible to get to the town fifteen miles away so their lives depended on the supplies on hand.

The animals were kept inside to protect them from the bitter cold. The corn in the bin was carefully measured out, and the hay from the mow supplemented with straw and cornstalks that the men chopped with their big corn knives. The only paths through the whiteness were the ones to the well and thence on to the stable, and to the woodpile. It was a long and disagreeable task for Thomas and Henry to draw water for the animals. To have made a path to the creek would have been impossible.

In the lean-to shed behind the house the girls laboriously

ground corn and wheat into coarse meal. This could be baked into bread or cooked and eaten with sorghum molasses, or with the milk from the two cows. One by one other supplies ran out, but there was plenty of grain, and a sufficient supply of butter, which the girls churned twice a week. A bit of dough saved from each batch of bread served as leavening for the next. It was a monotonous diet, but nourishing.

"Next year we'll have a plenty of other things to eat," said Hester. "I seed—I mean I saw—a whole passel of crab-apple trees on the hill. We can dry them, the apples I mean, not the trees. And there's blackberries. I saw the briars when I went to the creek one day. And there's bound to be strawberries and gooseberries and hickory nuts and persimmons."

"Are you going to dry persimmons?"

"No, I ain't simple enough to try that. But I'll show you! I'll put molasses with them and bile 'em up and make persimmon butter. It will keep in a stone jar in the shed. You'll see!"

"I'm willing to see, but please don't ask me to taste! Persimmons *without* sorghum are all I can stand. If I get any sugar next summer, I'm going to have some real jell."

"Jell is fine for comp'ny, but nothing can beat long sweetnin' for every day."

"What, may I ask, is 'long sweetnin'?"

"Why, any kind of 'lasses. Honest, didn't you know *that*, Sarah?"

"Honest, I'm that ignorant," said Sarah, a bit sarcastically. "I suppose you will be mixing it with pumpkins for pies."

"Yes, it's good!" answered Hester, not recognizing the sarcasm. "Oh, it's untellin' what I will do when spring comes, and then the summer when I can root in the gyarden, and fall when the nuts and 'simmons gets ripe. I crave to give time a shove!"

With the necessity for keeping indoors came longer periods of reading and discussion. Even when they were busy, the men weaving baskets or smoothing down the new furniture,

109

the women sewing or knitting, the talk would turn to the things they had been reading.

"What a great number of aspects there are to our relationship to God!" mused Thomas one day.

"What do you mean?" asked Henry.

"He has so many names, each revealing a different—what shall I say? A different—well, relationship is the only word that I can think of. Each of them ties us to Him in a different way."

"For instance?"

"I'll give you a few. Then you can think others up for yourselves. Think of the names He called Himself. He said He was the Bread of Life, the Vine, the Light of the World—"

"The Good Shepherd!"

"And the Way, the Truth, and the Life!"

"And the Water of Life."

"There must be a lot of others," Thomas said. "Let's keep a list. As we read we can add to it."

Day by day the list grew. They enlarged it to include the names others had called Him—Friend, Counselor, Mighty God, Everlasting Father, Prince of Peace, Immanuel, the Foundation, the Rock, the Resurrection, the Rose of Sharon, the Lily of the valley.

One evening Thomas had read the second chapter of I Timothy, and they had found new names.

"Mediator. What is that, Thomas?"

"Our Intercessor, Hettie, the One who works between us and a just God to bring about a reconciliation."

"And what's a ransom?"

"It is the price paid to release a captive from bondage."

"And He's our ransom?"

"Yes, He is. He paid that price with His life."

"And now we're free?"

"Forever. It is all paid and all Hell can't annul it."

A few nights later they encountered another phase of it that brought forth more questions. They had started the Book of Romans, and after the first phrase Henry said, "Remember, Thomas, how Professor Emerson used to say that the word *servant* should have been translated *slave*?"

"Yes, he never forgot to say that. That word really meant 'a bondman' or 'slave.'"

"A slave?" said Hester in horror. "Oh, I've seed slaves. Are we like that?"

"Yes, we should be. But slaves to the most loving Master in the world."

"But you said we were *free*. We air ransomed. How can we be slaves?"

"That's your question, Thomas," said Henry with a laugh. "And I'm glad it's not I who has to satisfy that question box of yours."

Thomas reached over and patted the dark head that leaned against his knee. "Don't let him tease you, my Hettie. We all need to think deeply of that very thing. It's puzzling, but here is how I see it. We *are* free. The ransom has been paid, and sin and death, our great enemies, are defeated. We have accepted the gift of freedom, or our salvation as we often call it. Now as children of God we have the *privilege* of voluntarily accepting Christ as our *Master*. If we sincerely do that, we become His servants, or slaves. I'm afraid not many of us do it."

"But He bought us, didn't He? Then we're not our own self's any more. We're His'n!"

"Yes, His—His eternal possession. That is, if we accept His substitution for us. For some reason that I can't explain, Hettie, He doesn't force it on anybody. He lets each of us choose."

"But if we *do* choose to let Him save us, then we belong to Him, don't we? And ifen we don't hand over ourselfs, we're just plain ole thieves!"

Henry and Sarah laughed at her vehemence, but Thomas smiled and tightened his arm around her shoulder.

111

"Yes, Hettie girl, in lives as well as in money, men continue to rob God."

After Henry and Sarah had climbed to the loft that night, Hester went about preparing for bed with a sober face. She fixed the sponge for the next day's bread and covered it with a wooden lid over which she placed a heavy blanket. It would never do for the sponge to get chilled. She looked at the box in the corner to see that the gray cat and the kittens were warm.

"Maybe by this time next year we'll be tucking in a little one of our own," said Thomas as he watched her.

Her eyes shone as they met his. "I hanker for one," she said quietly.

Just before Thomas put out the candle he drew her into his arms.

"What makes you so sober, Hettie? Is there something that troubles you?"

"No—o, not troubles, just kindly stirs me up. I don't aim to rob God, Thomas, and I'm wantin' to turn what's His own over to Him. I feel to let Him have what He bought. He paid a moughty proud, big price for something that ain't worth much, but ifen He wants me, I crave to pleasure Him. And I don't rightly know just how to do it."

Thomas held her closely for a moment without speaking, then huskily he whispered, "Me, too, Hettie. Let's tell Him so now."

Side by side they knelt by the big bed, and in a moment, more solemn than even their wedding hour, they yielded up to the Purchaser the lives He had bought.

Having been faced with Christ's ownership, the young people began to ponder His commands. As Master He could command. They must obey. They read carefully through the Gospels, marking each command as they came to it. Hester listed them all in her ledger.

"It can't be just straight-out orders that are have-to's,"

112

she said one day. "When we find something that pleasures Him, we must do that, too."

"Like what?" said Henry.

"Well, like all them blessed's. He didn't say we *had* to be meek, but you know it would make Him moughty proud and glad ifen we was—I mean were."

"Being meek isn't so easy."

"I know that. I didn't say it was easy. I never figured bein' meek was even very nice. But if He wants that, I can do hit!" When Hester became excited, the laboriously learned lessons in grammar and pronunciation were forgotten!

After a few more minutes of discussion the "blessed's" were all added to the list, and they widened their search to include the things they thought He would desire. They did not work hastily. Each addition was made after thoughful discussion of what obedience to it would mean to them. Henry and Sarah, although agreeing in general with the decisions, were inclined to think that Thomas and Hester were too literal in their interpretation of what a Christian's duty might be.

They often concluded their evenings by singing some of the hymns from the books that Thomas had brought with him. This was a special delight to Hester, who loved to sing but knew few songs. She had no knowledge of music as the others knew it, but she had a quick ear and retentive memory, and soon she could sing with the rest any hymn that she had heard before. Out from that snowbound cabin on those nights would float the strains of "Amazing Grace," "Come, Thou Fount of Every Blessing," "There Is a Fountain Filled with Blood," or some other old and loved hymn. One night Thomas requested that Henry sing, "A Mighty Fortress Is Our God" in German, and Hester wept at the glorious tones although she did not understand a word. But the hymn she loved best and adopted as her own was Charles Wesley's "Father, Son, and Holy Ghost." One verse became her life's commitment.

> Take my soul and body's powers;
> Take my memory, mind and will,

All my goods and all my hours,
    All I know and all I feel.
All I think or speak or do,
    Take my heart, but make it new!

One night Sarah, who had been homesick all day, asked as they closed the Bible, "Can't we sing, 'Blest Be the Tie That Binds,' tonight? I need to be reminded that our fellowship is 'like to that above.'"

Touched by her wistful sadness, they realized that the hard life they were living was immeasurably more difficult for her than for the others. Henry reached for her one hand while Hester clasped the other. Then Hester, not wanting Thomas left out, drew him to her on her other side, and the four—shut in a snowbound cabin in a strange, new land—sang with full hearts in a bond of fellowship that was in truth, like to that above. Each night after that they ended the evening with that act of worship.

In early March the warm sun melted the snow so that Henry and Thomas could resume the building. The girls proved capable helpers, and soon the new cabin was ready. For the last time they stood together and sang. Then Henry and Sarah followed the path through the woods to their own home.

Chapter Seventeen

HESTER DID NOT FIND TIME to write much in her diary that summer. From early morning until darkness they were busy in the fields. Thomas and the oxen plowed the tough sod, and after them Hester would drive their one horse dragging a heavy log with great wooden teeth to break up the clods and clear the ground of grass roots. Back and forth, back and forth, stopping every few feet to take the clumps of roots out of the teeth and pile them to one side where Thomas could find them later and remove them. At night they were so tired that they would almost fall asleep over their supper.

After the ground was prepared, the corn must be planted. Thomas would walk ahead with a thick, pointed stick in his hand, punching a hole in the ground at every step. Behind him Hester came, dropping three grains of corn in each hole, and then stepping on it to cover it as she went on to the next. Thomas carried the heavy bag of seed over his shoulder, and at the end of each row he replenished the supply in Hester's basket. Day after day they toiled, and so slow was the process that by the time they had finished the big field, the first rows had strong sprouts. Already the small grains which had been sown as soon as the snow was gone were fields of green.

A garden had to be made, the hens set on nests of eggs, and soon the strawberries were showing pink on the hillsides. The corn must be hoed, and it was a wearisome task with the tough grass roots persisting in their growth. The weeds and grass in the garden seemed to grow faster than the beans and corn did. Cows must be milked, butter churned, bread baked. Fruit and berries were gathered from the woods and hills and dried in the hot sun. For the fortnightly washing, water had to be carried from the creek and heated in a big kettle in the yard. Such ironing as had to be done, was done with an iron heated in the coals of the fireplace. There were no hours of idleness. For many weeks at a time Hester and Sarah never saw each other except for the hour on Sunday morning when the families for miles about met in one of the houses for worship.

Occasionally, however, there would be a few minutes stolen from other things to write a page in the ledger—a page that told her great-great-great-grandson five generations later something of the toil and struggle his pioneer ancestors had paid for the winning of the land, and a great deal of the spiritual growth of the mountain girl who wrote it. For from the night that she realized at what a price she had been "boughten," she never faltered in her allegiance to the Master who had paid that price. She could not write one page without telling of some new experience with Him or some new lesson from His Book. As she grew spiritually, her mind developed and her education, under Thomas' patient and kindly tutoring, advanced.

Another winter came. There was more of companionship, for there were now more than a dozen families in the valley. There was also more food in the house and barn. During these winter days the women sewed and cooked, read over and over again the few books they owned, exchanged books with the other families, and almost gloated over the leisurely life they led. Why, there was an hour or so every day when they could do as they pleased.

"I'd like to save up some of this spare time for use next summer, like we saved the vegetables and fruit for this winter.

I'd like some dried hours to use next July when the corn needs hoeing," Hester wrote.

In January Sarah's and Henry's baby was born, a lovely little girl with a rosebud face and Sarah's red-gold hair. But she did not breathe in spite of the desperate efforts of Hester and Mrs. Morgan while they waited for Thomas to return with the doctor. It was Hester who bathed the still little form and robed it in the lace-trimmed dress over which Sarah had spent countless hours. At the mother's tearful insistence it was laid for a few minutes in her arms. Outside, Thomas and Sam Morgan were making the little coffin.

"Tell them to line it with the train of my wedding dress," Sarah whispered through trembling lips. "Mother said I was foolish to bring it, but I told her I'd find some use for it."

It was Hester who stayed with Sarah and held her in her arms while Thomas and Henry and the Morgans climbed to the top of the only hill on the Putney farm, where the men had made ready the earth for the return to it of this first pioneer baby.

["I can see that scene," thought Dr. Andrew Lewis as he read. "I've been through it so many times in the Congo—the plain homemade coffin, the quick burial—it was the same here as there. I know how they felt."]

On a bright day in February Henry came past with Sarah wrapped warmly in blankets in the box of the homemade sled drawn by the oxen.

"We're going up to the hill, Hester, and I'd like for you to go with us. I don't know how Sarah will take it, and I'll feel better if you are there."

Thomas laid aside the harness he was repairing and went with them. The four of them stood silently by the little mound which was barely discernible through the snow. Sarah sobbed quietly on Henry's shoulder, while the tears ran unheeded down his cheeks. Hester turned to the shelter of Thomas' arms, knowing that in his mind, as in hers, was the question, "Will our baby be up here soon?"

Then Sarah surprised them all with one of the unexpected changes of thought which characterized her.

"Do you know what I want?"

"No," said Henry, wiping his eyes, "but whatever it is, you can have it."

"I want a church. They were talking the other week about building a schoolhouse and using it for a church for awhile. I want a church here, right by my baby's grave."

Henry and Thomas promised that it should be done, and before Henry unhitched the oxen he went to spread the word among the neighbors that he was giving an acre of land there for a churchyard, and asking the help of all in preparing the logs. So it was, that before the work in the fields began, there arose under the trees on the hill a little log church, the first in the valley.

In March Hester's and Thomas' son was born—a frail, thin little fellow who would not thrive on any food that could be procured for him, but who persistently refused to let loose of life. He was dark and tiny and wrinkled, and Thomas secretly thought him the most unpromising morsel of humanity he had ever seen.

"He probably looks like me," said Hester. "But I prayed he'd act like you, so he will be a fine man. I forgot to pray that he'd look like you, too."

During all that summer it seemed to Hester that there was never a cessation of his thin crying. Whether in her arms, or in his cradle, or in a big basket at the edge of the field where she worked with Thomas, he kept up his wailing. When he fell asleep from sheer exhaustion, his parents found opportunity for a few hours of rest themselves, but ever afterwards, when Hester looked back to that summer she could not remember sleeping at all. It seemed that she had stayed awake from March to October, when for some reason no one could discover, little Andrew ceased his crying and began to enjoy the world into which he had been born. The winter came on, their third in this land, and they had time to enjoy the baby. As he grew plump and playful Hester felt that her heart would burst from joy in the possession of him. One night as they looked at him sleeping in his cradle, Hester spoke what was in her heart.

"He pleasures me more every day. My heart keens for Sarah Putney. I pray everly that she will get to keep her next baby."

"I do, too. I felt almost guilty when I saw Henry rocking little Andrew's cradle the other day. A baby is the best thing God ever made!"

"But it's a moughty load on folks, too. I have a heavy feel when I think that when I borned little Andrew I borned a soul that will live on some place forever. It trembles me!"

"We will just have to turn him over to the Lord and then do our best to raise him for that Lord. Don't you remember we gave him to God before he was born?"

"Yes, I do, but I have to keep giving him over again every day. It's a dreadful thing, Thomas, to know that you've started something that you can't ever end. We borned Andrew, but even if we wanted to, we couldn't end his life. It will just go on and on. You believe that, don't you, Thomas?"

"Certainly I do."

"That's why we just have to keep letting loose of him and turning him over to God. You know we just cain't raise him right our ownselfs. God has to do it. If He does it, Andrew will spend his 'forever' in Heaven."

As spring came on again Hester grew gravely concerned about Sarah. There just must not be another little grave up on the hill. She got out the big "medicine book" Thomas had brought with him, and studied diligently to discover any way she might help her friend. She insisted that Thomas keep the horse ready at all times for the fifteen-mile ride for the doctor.

In April another little girl came to the Putneys, a baby so like the other that it healed the last bit of the pain left from the year before. She was a healthy, chubby baby, and

Hester and Thomas were hardly less happy at her safe arrival than her parents were.

As they walked back to their own cabin after seeing the little one tucked into its cradle and the mother resting with a happy smile on her face, Thomas said, shifting his heavy son to his other arm, "Don't you think this is the time for the Doxology? Sing it, Hester."

And Hester sang. Henry and Sarah heard it and felt its echo in their hearts.

["I've felt that way myself, when a baby is safely ushered into the world," thought Dr. Lewis. "I wonder why we are so happy over it? The road ahead is usually tough for the poor things. Yet the happiest people in the world are new mothers, and the proudest are the new dads." Then he winced at the realization that such pride might never be his.]

Chapter Eighteen

As THE YEARS PASSED, they seemed to go as if on wings. They were full of hard work, of deep joy, and of heavy grief. Other families came in over the mountains and across the great river. As Hester stood on her doorstep on a winter day when the trees were bare, she could see the smoke from a dozen chimneys. A schoolhouse stood at the crossroads where the highway from the South crossed the trail that came down from the hills. The log church was enlarged and covered by white weatherboarding. In the yard at the side there were a score of graves. Most of these were of babies. Pioneer life is always hardest on the little ones.

["I remember what we studied of the infant death rate in those days," mused Dr. Lewis. "It was almost fifty per cent."]

Sarah and Henry had laid a tiny son by the little daughter, and Hester and Thomas had three short mounds to tend in summer. Hester was not able to put into her diary a record of the grief she felt at the loss of her babies. There were only a few short lines.

"I'm not grudging You having them, Lord. They are really Yours and I was just borroying them. But my mother heart aches and You will have to bear me up. Don't let Thomas and me take our eyes off of You!"

There was no time to grieve in idleness. The work must be done, and in each home there were other children to be loved and cared for. The Putneys had three boys besides the lovely little Kate, and Henry joked about retiring to let the sturdy youngsters run the farm. Andrew Lewis was a tall, quiet boy of twelve, and Mary, his brown-haired sister, a serious sweet-faced girl of ten. After these two there had been the three who had been taken from them. Then had come Benny, who at three years old was the pride and delight of the family.

When he had come triumphantly through that dangerous "second summer" that took such heavy toll of children in those days, Hester had said with shining eyes as she watched him romp with the puppy, "He's just a blessed gift from Heaven. God knows I didn't grudge Him the others. I don't know why it had to be, but I trusted Him to take care of them. And then He sent Benny along to us to remind us every day of His love. With Andrew, our good boy, and Mary, our sweet girl, and Benny just a big chunk of sunshine, we couldn't ask anything more!"

Hester herself had changed in the years since she rode into the valley and sang the Doxology out of sheer joy at being alive. Some of the exuberance of spirit had gone, but the diary revealed that in its place had come a calmness of soul, born of trust in God that shone out of her eyes and illumined the tanned and wind-roughened face. In the pages of the diary there was a sketch of her as she appeared at that time. It was roughly done in charcoal and signed, "To Hester from the would-be artist, Sarah."

[As Dr. Lewis looked at it he thought, "The world lost a real artist when Sarah buried her talents here." For in spite of the crudity of the sketch and of the blurring of the lines over the years, the spirit of the subject still shone out of the pictured face.]

There were other changes, too, that would have been apparent to those around her. Her speech had changed from that of an untutored mountain girl to that of a woman who had read, not widely but deeply, good books. In the diary her handwriting had grown smoother and more regular without losing its evidence of strength, and the words and phrasings took on the characteristics of those books. Some of them had

122

the dignity and beauty of the Scriptures that were her best source of not only spiritual food but instruction in the arts which Henry, Sarah, and Thomas had learned in school. Long ago her feeling of inferiority to the others had vanished. She had her Lord, as much of Him as she was able to contain, and who had more? Again and again in the diary was recorded her prayer, "Don't *ever* let me lose sight of my Master! Don't let anything or anybody be between me and Him. Never let me forget that He bought me!"

With it all there was in her a keen, droll wit that showed through the writings in the most unlooked-for places. Dr. Andrew Lewis laughed aloud at times over the drollery even while his throat constricted at the poignancy of the story.

It was during the fall and winter after Andrew was twelve that the "big house" was built. The rooms were of log with a great loft overhead, a loft that was reached by a stairway rather than a ladder and that was divided to make rooms for the children. The old house still stood at the back where it could be used for storage and for a summer kitchen. Here the cooking was done during the hot days when an extra degree of heat would have made the living rooms unbearable. Hester could put her bread in the brick oven and, while it baked, could sit in the "settin' room" in almost unbelievable comfort while she sewed her carpet rags. It seemed to her as she considered her blessings that the lines had indeed fallen unto her in pleasant places.

It was during these years that Hester started the ministry that was to continue as long as she was able to be about. It became noised about the countryside that "Hester Lewis had a knack for the carin' for sick folks. And she's as good as a doctor when the babies come." So wherever there was need, she went. Oftentimes the call would come in the night and, leaving the children to Thomas' care, she would fare forth on horseback, following the messenger who had brought the summons. Many times it would be to minister in a home that was strange to her. Often she found she had to fight ignorance and dirt as well as disease. The young doctor who had moved to the nearest village learned to depend on her for all the assistance that doctors of a century later could receive from a full corps of nurses. Sarah questioned the wisdom of this widespread service.

"You'll be carrying all sorts of sickness home to your own children," she remonstrated.

"That did worry me at first," Hester admitted. "But somebody has to help folks. And I figured that I was mighty belittlin' to God if I thought He couldn't take care of mine while I was out helping His folks."

Her trust was not misplaced, for the diary had no record of any harm to the Lewis family from these contacts.

There was another phase to the ministry in which Thomas also had a share. Back in the hills a settlement had sprung up which had a bad reputation among the valley dwellers. The people were generally shiftless and considered unsavory of character. It was here that Hester's war against dirt and ignorance was waged. At first Thomas protested against her going there at all.

"It's not safe for you, my Hettie. It is quite thoroughly understood that most of those people have been run out of other communities because they aren't fit to live among decent folks. They wouldn't be sick all the time if they would clean up and live as they should. So long as they persist in their careless filth, you can't do them any permanent good. Next time they send for you, you just tell them your husband and children need you at home!"

Being an obedient wife, Hester tried to accede to his request. But her heart was tender toward the children who lived in this sordid place, and when she heard that some of them were ill, she could not refuse aid. Thomas, shaking his head in resignation, insisted on going with her, and while she labored in the sickroom, he talked to the men outside. This became a pattern for the trips.

One night as they drove home long after midnight he said

to her, "Hettie, I had an experience tonight that I will never forget. I was talking to old Pete Hicks while you were in the house, and I found there a soul so barren and hungry it made me sick. For the first time in my life I had the privilege of telling the Gospel story to a person who had never heard the name of Jesus Christ except in an oath. I can't get over it."

"Oh, Thomas, what an experience! What did he say? Did he believe?"

"Not yet, but I'm going back. He didn't scoff. Just kept saying, 'I never heerd that afore,' as if it were unbelievable. Will you pray with me, Hettie? I *must* win him for the Lord."

"Indeed I will, Thomas! Wouldn't it be wonderful if Christ would come into that community and change it?"

"He could," Thomas said slowly. "But I reckon He will have to work through someone like you and me. Maybe He wants us to do something for souls as well as bodies up there."

"I know what we'll do! We will start a school on Sunday afternoons when folks aren't working.

"They would be glad to quit their work *any* day," interpolated Thomas."

"I could teach the women, and you could talk to the men. Maybe Betsy Morgan would go along and teach the children. Let's do it, Thomas!"

She was so excited that Thomas grabbed her arm as if he feared she might jump from the two-wheeled cart and start back to the settlement, waken the inhabitants, and begin her work at once.

Thomas was slower to accept this idea. "It would be very hard on you, Hettie. You've always called Sunday afternoon your time for resting, the only time in the week when you didn't feel that something had to be done at once. You can't spare that rest time, my girl."

"Listen, Thomas Lewis! What do a few hours of rest for me mean as compared to the welfare of the souls of those folks up the creek? Why, Thomas, they're *lost*! Christ wants us to go to them, I know He does. We're His servants, and we have to go when He says so! He'll take care of our bodies. Even if we wear out for Him, we will only be doing what He says! I think so much of how awful it would be to be lost. I got lost when I was a little girl. I was in the woods alone all night before they found me. Even yet I dream about it. I can't stand for everyone not to have a chance to be *found*. I have to do all I can to give everybody that chance."

"All right, my Hettie. If God has said, 'Go!' to you, I'll not stand in the way. In fact, I'll go along. I'm not much of a teacher, but I'll do my best. With Him, it can't fail."

That was the beginning of the Sunday school "up the creek," a labor for the Lord that, in the course of the years, changed the little community from a place that was a byword for all things evil, to one whose people, though they would always be poor in this world's goods, loved and feared the Lord and sent their young folks unashamedly into the world.

[In that same place Sid Lewis and his wife were carrying on the work, counting it all joy to sacrifice the Sunday afternoon rest that the Gospel might be given out "to these also."]

Chapter Nineteen

ANDREW AND MARY went to the crossroads to school, trudging the mile and a half over the dusty road or riding together on Andrew's pony, Prince, and racing with Kate Putney with small Jim behind her on the way home. It was one of Mary's grievances that Kate almost always won, and she felt sure that Andrew purposely let her do it. Mary *knew* Prince could go faster if Andrew would let him. Why, he seemed to *want* Kate to win!

"What makes him act so silly when she's around?" she asked Hester as they did the dishes one night. "It's no fun to race unless you try to win. He's so *queer* about her. Why, he misses words in spelling that I know he can spell, just to let her get ahead of him. I don't think that is very smart!"

Hester laughed as she answered her little daughter, "He has always been that way about Katie, Mary. He seems to think she is some kind of fairy, not like the rest of us at all."

"Well, she isn't, Ma," said Mary soberly. "She is as selfish as anything and she sometimes tells fibs, but not when Andrew is near. I don't like her much. She acts as if I were only a little girl, and I'm as near her age as Andrew is!"

"Yes, but you're on the wrong end of the age line, honey. You're a year younger while Brother is a year older. That makes a lot of difference to Katie."

"It doesn't to me. Sometimes I feel like getting real cross with her! But I never do," she added hastily.

"I'm sure you don't, and I know I can trust you not to do

anything that would make Mother ashamed of her big girl. Just wait a few years and the difference in age between you and Katie won't be noticeable. In fact, she might be claiming to be younger than you!"

"Whatever would make her do a silly thing like that? Nobody would ever want to be younger. Why, I can hardly wait until I grow up and marry Dick Morgan. I hope we have ten little babies and that they all look like Benny!"

Hester took the towel and hung it on the line in the back kitchen, saying as she did so, "Don't grow too fast, Mary Mavourneen. I can't spare my little girl yet."

It was spring again and a week of torrential rains had flooded the streams and filled even the roadside ditches with swiftly flowing rivulets. The water was fascinating to little Benny. He watched the twigs and bits of debris swirl and float past, and added to it by throwing in all the sticks he could find. Twice he was discovered on his way to the creek at the foot of the back pasture. Thomas at last tied the gate shut.

"It will have to stay that way until the water goes down. He can't be trusted. It's too muddy for the cows to be out so we won't have to use that gate."

On a Saturday afternoon when the children were out of school, Hester was kept in bed by a return of the "ager" that was a continual menace to the pioneers. From chills to fever, then chills again, then more fever! It was a weakening and painful ailment that took its toll of strength and sometimes of life.

Thomas and Andrew had driven into the village, and Mary was busy in the kitchen. Benny was napping on the "settle." Hester had fallen into a restless sleep, but wakened when Thomas and Andrew came in.

"Where are the children?" asked Thomas, placing his hand on her forehead to note the amount of fever.

"They're—why Mary's in the kitchen and the baby's asleep."

"No, neither of them is here. Guess Mary took Benny with

her to gather the eggs. I'll go and see. I got them the striped peppermints I promised."

Thomas and Andrew went out and Hester turned restlessly in her bed. Minute by minute she listened for the noisy return. At the continuing silence she felt a wave of panic sweep over her. Had something happened to her little ones? She dressed in clumsy haste and ran from the door without waiting for a wrap. Through the chicken house and the barn she went, but they were deserted. Then to the back lot where tracks in the soft ground showed that the man and boy had climbed the fence. She saw them running toward the creek. She never knew how she got across the fence and down the lane. She caught up to them as they were starting in the dusk along the creek bank.

"Hettie, girl, you shouldn't have come," Thomas said gently.

"Oh, I had to! Why did you come down here? Did you see them?"

"We saw their tracks. Benny must have slipped out of the house and climbed the fence. Mary missed him and followed. Her tracks are on top of his."

"Oh, my babies! Dear God, help them!"

They found them at last down where the line fence crossed the creek and made a barrier to catch the logs and debris that floated down. Mary's arms were tightly clasped around the little brother she had tried in vain to save, and her brown locks were tangled with his golden ones.

The next weeks were always like a dream to Hester. For many days she lay near death. She dreamed of a country more beautiful than any words could describe, where Mary played with four little toddlers around her and where a soft light glowed over all with indescribable glory. In her ears were the rich tones of a Voice, "The Lamb is the Light thereof."

She wanted to join Mary and the babies. How she would love to gather them all into her hungry arms! But behind

129

her she could hear Andrew crying, and Thomas' voice saying over and over, "My Hettie, my Hettie."

Again and again the dream came. Mary would turn and give her a smile, and the babies reached out chubby arms to her. Always she longed to enter into the lovely place, and always there was the call from Thomas and Andrew to hold her back.

`One morning she wakened to feel the warm sun streaming in through the window and to hear Sarah Putney's voice in the kitchen.

When Thomas came in later he kissed her, while the tears streamed down his cheeks, and he cried brokenly, "Oh, Hettie girl, it's Heaven to see you smile at me again!"

For several days she lay thus, not speaking unless questioned, and appearing only half-conscious at times. But at last there came a day when she called for Thomas, and when he came and knelt by her bed, she took his face between her hands.

"Forgive me, Thomas. I have given you a bad time, I know. But you don't have to worry any more. I'm getting well now, and I've been lying here thinking. It's all right about the children, dear. God gave us a lot of happiness in them, and He's just taken them back now to care for until we can be with them. I saw them in my dreams and they are happier than we could ever make them. And I'm not going to grudge them to Him. It's all right with you, too, isn't it, Thomas?"

"It's all right, Hester, it's all right. His way is best," he answered huskily, and matched her trembling smile with one of his own.

When Sarah came in with the bowl of broth she had been making, she found them planning together with Andrew for the flower garden he wanted to make in the side yard.

"How can you be so resigned?" Sarah asked some weeks later as one Sunday morning after church the two women slipped away from the men to visit the graves on the hillside. "I couldn't stand it if I were you. Why, I get sick when I think of my two babies here, and you've lost so much more. I can't understand you!"

Hester stooped to pull up a dandelion that had grown on one little mound, and said softly, "I guess I couldn't stand it if I had to do it myself. But a long time ago, Sarah, I just let loose of myself. Thomas and I, together one night, gave ourselves completely to the Lord. I don't mean we made a gift to Him. We couldn't do that. We just let loose of what He had bought and let Him have possession. We've never gone back on that deal, but we've learned that it is a process that has to be continued. It's hard not to try to take hold again. Always we're having to let loose of new things our hearts would cling to. But He makes us able to do it. We've grown a lot in these fifteen years, I hope, Sarah. Then, we gave Him ourselves. Now, we want to gladly give Him all we own—our goods, our farm, our children, too, for whatever He wants to do with them."

She stopped for a minute, then burst forth as if compelled, "But it hurts, Sarah! No one who hasn't been through it can know the pain of it. I had planned to give Mary all the pretties and good times I never had for myself. She was so sweet! When I listen for her singing and for Benny's happy little laugh, and there's only that awful stillness with me alone in the house, I think I'll die! Then I'm ashamed. I'm really not alone. I tell the Lord I'm sorry, and He comes and brings peace again. He knows I'm not grudging the little ones to Him!"

Sarah wiped her eyes and answered wistfully, "I think you're wonderful. I wish I could give my children to God like that. Maybe I wouldn't spoil them so badly if I could think they were His. But I'm afraid of what He'd do if I gave them to Him. I've just *got* to hold them tight. If He let anything happen to Katie, I know I'd die!"

They walked slowly back to where the men waited. The Putneys drove off in the smart new carriage that had been Henry's anniversary gift to Sarah, and the Lewises followed in the wagon that would have been the better for a new coat of paint. After her friends had turned off toward their own home, Hester's eyes still followed them.

"Are you wishing you had a carriage like that?" Thomas asked soberly.

"No, I'm feeling sorry for Sarah Putney. She never in this world will know real joy. She just can't let go and trust God. You know in class today the lesson was about Caleb. There isn't much told about him in the Bible, but that little tells a whole lot. Caleb 'wholly followed the Lord,' Thomas. Isn't that a tremendous thing to say about anybody?"

"Truly tremendous!"

"A person couldn't do that without trusting. Poor Sarah just can't trust. It isn't any wonder that Caleb got what he asked for, is it?"

["And no wonder that Hester Lewis was remembered for generations as a woman who also followed Him," thought Dr. Lewis.]

Chapter Twenty

N O MORE CHILDREN came into the Lewis home. Andrew alone was left to them, and on him they poured out their love without measure. He looked like Hester with his dark eyes and unruly hair, but his quiet serenity and unruffled patience were like Thomas. He loved his studies; and his parents, seeing his aptitude for learning, were torn between two desires: one, to have him on the farm with them, the other, to see him in some profession—minister, physician, lawyer, they did not care which. Alternately they pictured him in each.

"He could be any of them and still live with us," said Hester one evening as they sat on the porch waiting for him to return from the Putney's. "The village is only five miles away, and he could ride back and forth on horseback."

Thomas laughed. "Don't forget, Mother, that there may not be an opening for him in the village, no matter what profession he chooses. I'm afraid that if we insist on having him with us, he will have to be a farmer. Don't forget, dear, that we gave him to the Lord. Let's let Him guide."

"Oh," she cried contritely, "I'm wrong, of course. One would think that by this time I'd have learned my lesson! I'll not try to hold him or influence him. I'll leave him to the Lord."

Never again did she speak of any plans. She did, however, spend more time every day on her knees in the bedroom. At other times she went about her work at home or in the homes of the neighbors with a calm face that was a mirror of the calm soul within. In her diary on one of those days she wrote a verse of the song she had learned long ago.

> Take my soul and body's powers;
>> Take my memory, mind and will,
> All my goods and all my hours,
>> All I know and all I feel.
> All I think or speak or do,
>> Take my heart, but make it new!

After the young people had finished with the district school, they rode into the village to the academy that had been started there. Kate Putney, quick at learning, had overcome the difference in age and finished at the little schoolhouse the same year Andrew did. Every morning for the next four school years they met at the crossroad and rode to school together. Kate was inclined to be a bit of a princess, demanding homage from all about her. This homage Andrew had paid her all her life. There was a family story that the first time he had seen her he had laid a bedraggled dandelion on her blanket. He had been bringing her offerings ever since, flowers from the garden, fruits from the orchards, nuts from the woods, and whatever other treasures he could procure. Kate accepted them all, as a queen accepts her due from her subjects.

She gave him something in return, however. She gave him the adoration of her heart, and neither her brothers nor her parents dared to tease her about Andrew. Before they had finished the academy, it was understood by both families that Andrew and Kate would marry. They agreed to wait a couple of years until Kate should have had a chance to go back East to the school her mother had attended, and until Andrew should have made a start on his career.

It seemed evident that career was to be the farm. He loved his books, but best of all, he loved the farm and the life they lived there. He was apologetic when he told of his decision, for he had felt that his parents expected him to choose a profession. But he knew the farm was where he belonged,

134

and here he must stay. Hester felt a thrill of joy as she realized that he would be left to them. They could build another house on the other side of the garden. Now that Thomas had bought that quarter-section across the creek the farm would provide for two families.

"I'd have let him go if You had asked it, Lord," she whispered. "But I do thank You for leaving him with us."

For two years Andrew worked away on the farm, saving all that he could of his share of the crops and livestock, and making plans for a house that would be nice enough for a princess. Kate finished at her eastern school and came home. When her brothers teased her about not catching an "eastern beau," she answered pettishly, "I wish you'd be still! There's only one man I care about, and you know who that is. I get tired of your foolishness!"

To Sarah and Henry Putney, and Hester and Thomas Lewis, who had come over the mountains together to share life in a strange, raw land, and who had gone with each other through fair weather and foul, through joy and deep sorrow, it seemed a part of God's wise plan that their children should marry. To Andrew and Kate the future lay before them as the fulfillment of a dream that had been shared as long as they could remember.

In the late fall when the crops were all in and the long evenings were free, itinerant preachers often came for two weeks of "protracted meetings." In a country community, held within itself by winter roads that were almost impassable and forced to make its own entertainment during the months that gave them any leisure for amusements, these meetings were an event. No one who was able to get there by horseback, sleigh, wagon, or on foot would ever miss.

The preacher who came the fall after Kate had returned from the East was a gaunt, long-haired apostle, who preached with a fire and vigor that seemed to be gradually consuming his frail frame. He thought of himself as a voice crying in this western wilderness. He saw not only America, but the

135

world as a field white unto the harvest, with many portions of it entirely unmanned by laborers. He had read avidly all that he could find of the opening up of missionary work in China, India, and Africa. He was too old to go himself, but he longed to see an army of young people going forth into the work. During his two weeks' stay, he preached the message of salvation, but he also in every service emphasized the responsibility of Christians to be about the Master's business of taking the Gospel to the whole world.

To most of his listeners this was a new thought. They were in a pioneer land themselves. Their lives were full of hard work and there was neither time nor means to give to folks on the other side of the globe. They did not get much news even from the churches on the other side of the mountains. They had become so engrossed in their own problems and heavy burdens that they had forgotten that the command, "Go ye!" was to them as well as to any other group of the Lord's followers. When faced with their obligation, they were made sober and thoughtful. Andrew resolved that he would give all the money from one of his fat hogs to the preacher and ask him to send it where it would help to get the Word to the heathen. Kate, when she heard of it, added the money her uncle had given her for some nice dishes. The preacher taught them a new song, and night after night the strains of "From Greenland's Icy Mountains" rang out on the frosty air.

In the last meeting the entire service was devoted to missions, and the congregation sat spellbound as they heard of the work of the self-forgetful men and women who were carrying the Light to the dark places of the earth. There were almost unbelievable stories of sacrifice and heroism.

"But they are so few, that little group of soldiers that are battling on the front line!" the old man cried passionately. "Why didn't I realize forty years ago that when the Lord said, 'Go,' He meant it, and that everyone should go or show good excuse why he can't. Don't wait until you hear some clarion voice from Heaven, you young folks! Get ready to go unless you are called to stay home!"

He finished with a plea for volunteers, not for the mission field, but for complete consecration in any place or work where the Lord should ask.

"If you've never yielded your whole being to Him, you have never fully lived," he said. "You will never know the fullness of joy and peace that Christ has for His own until you let go of self and let Him take over. That is what I am asking you to do now. Don't come unless you mean that you will go wherever and do whatever He asks. It may be in India, Africa, or China, or in the islands of the sea. It may be in the tents and tepees of our American Indians, or into the burning heat and icy blizzards of our western plains. Or it may be here at home to toil and pray and give that others may go. All that I'm asking is that you be willing to do whatever He says, to go wherever He sends, to be whatever He wants. Will you come? Let's sing!"

He started the song and they all joined in. Many of the young people were standing with bowed heads. Up in the front row with the choir, Andrew and Kate stood side by side. Hester watched them anxiously. It seemed to her that she could not stand it if her son did not answer such a call. Yet if he did, what would it mean? For a moment she almost wished the preacher had not brought such a message. She wanted to be back in the security of her home where she had had sweet fellowship with the Lord, but where such problems as this had not entered. Then with a silent prayer, "Dear Lord, forgive me, and take him if You will," she made her surrender.

Andrew was looking pleadingly at Kate, but her head was turned away. He touched her arm, but she did not move, and at last without her Andrew stepped forward and gave his hand to the old man who stood waiting. Dick Morgan was but a step behind him. Then Ruthie Barnes came hesitantly from her place beside big Tod Hendricks.

"Bless these young people for coming. But there should be more. There should be some of you older ones. Surely not all of you have already taken such a step. I'm not asking you to go to a foreign land. I'm just asking you to be *willing* to go or to be or to do as He says. If you've never made such a promise to Him, do it now. He wants every one of you."

Several more came, among them John Barnes, Ruthie's father. For years, ever since his wife had been taken from him, he had been bitter and rebellious. Now the tears on his cheeks told of submission to that decree. After the last verse of a song, the meeting was closed with a prayer of dedication.

There was no opportunity for Hester to speak to Andrew then. Nor did she desire to. What had happened tonight was so sacred that she wanted to be in her own home with Thomas and Andrew when they discussed it. She smiled at her son as she met his eyes above the crowd about him, then she turned away with Thomas.

It was past midnight when they heard him drive into the yard. They were waiting, for they knew they could not sleep. For two hours they had been talking about what this might mean, and they were ready to meet it.

He entered quietly and stood looking at them, his face pale and his eyes red-rimmed. He held out a hand to each of them as if to draw them into sympathy with his purpose.

"Mother—Father—I had to do it! You wanted me to, didn't you? I couldn't stay in my seat. It would have been like telling Him I wasn't His. I couldn't do that!"

"Of course you couldn't, son," said Thomas. "We would have been a sad pair if you had failed Him. We thank God—"

"But what does it mean, my boy?" asked Hester. "Has a call come?"

He looked at her out of anguished eyes.

"I have to go to the field—I don't know where. But I have to go. It isn't right nor fair for us to have so much and

138

those others not to even get a chance to hear about Him. I *have* to go! But—but—Katie—oh, how can I say it?"

"She won't go, lad," said Hester. It was not a question. They *knew*. Andrew flung himself down on the old "settle" and cried as he had not done since that long-ago day when he had thought his mother was dying. Thomas stood awkwardly patting the rumpled hair, and Hester knelt with her arms around Him. She knew without being told what the scene between the young people had been. She remembered that Sarah had said that she could not give her children to God for fear of what He might do with them. And Kate, now, could not yield because she was not willing to let God do with her as He would.

The days passed in sad procession. There was no drawing back on Andrew's part, but the relinquishment of all the plans that had been so happily made was not easy. He went about his work quietly, as industrious and efficient as ever, but the whistle or song which had usually told Hester where he was, was heard no more. He did not mention Kate again, nor did his parents.

Sarah came over one day when she had seen Thomas and Andrew driving past on their way to the village. She was a saddened Sarah, and approached the subject that was uppermost in the thoughts of both of them with hesitation and embarrassment.

"You won't hold it against Katie, will you, Hester?" she asked timidly. "It has been hard for her, too. It isn't easy to change plans that have meant so much to you. After all, it wasn't she who changed. And she has cried herself sick over it."

"I wouldn't want her to do that," said Hester, ignoring the implication that Andrew was to be blamed. "Each of them had to make his own decision, and we shan't criticize. It is hard for us all."

"Yes, it is. Henry and I feel as if there had been a death

in the family. Even the boys feel badly. We had all thought for so long that Katie and Andrew—"

She could not go on for a few minutes, then she spoke almost defiantly, "She *couldn't* have done differently, Hester. To pledge herself to go wherever God might send her! That was too much. I was praying she wouldn't go. I couldn't stand it if Katie went as a missionary!"

Hester's heart ached for her friend. After twenty-five years of close fellowship, they seemed now to be almost strangers. They had no common language in which to discuss this problem.

When Sarah rose to leave, she said pleadingly, "This won't make a difference between you and me, will it, Hester?"

"Of course not. We've been friends too long to let anything come between us. We will just ask God to bless our children. Then we will leave them in His hands and go on as before."

She watched Sarah go back along the woods path, and thought sadly, "Oh, if she just *could* leave Katie with Him! But she's afraid to. So she tries to work things out by herself. It won't do. It never does. God help them all!"

Chapter Twenty-one

SARAH LEFT THE NEXT WEEK to visit her sister in Virginia, taking Kate with her. Andrew, with Dick Morgan, began to make plans for further schooling in the fall. Thomas and Hester were interested in every development and often the four sat far into the night, discussing the information they had gathered about different schools, and trying to decide which would be best. The choice narrowed down to three, then when word came of a missionary conference to be held at the college in Alton, the two lads rode horseback one hundred and fifty miles to attend. They came home with shining eyes and hearts aglow. There was no more hesitation. They had enrolled in Sheffield College and would enter in the September class.

Hester and Thomas rejoiced to see that when they were engrossed in these plans, Andrew would regain his normal, happy outlook on life. True, when alone at some task or when at church with the other young people, he would sink back into the despondency that the thought of Kate always brought, and the pain in his eyes made his parents' hearts ache. They could only pray that time and an engrossing interest would bring healing.

Winter changed to spring, spring gave place to summer, and the boys were counting the weeks until they should leave. Hester had sewed for months, patiently making by hand the six shirts, six sets of underwear, and the one new suit Andrew would have. She read in a paper that a New England farmer had invented a queer machine that would do stitching, but the writer said it was even slower than hand stitching. Hester was sure the man must be an impractical dreamer. No machine could ever do a thing like that in a way that would be of any real value to a busy woman. So she worked early and late, putting into the plain garments all the care she had hoped to put some day into a daughter's trousseau. And Andrew dreamed of a day when, the schooling finished, he should travel through Congo jungles or Indian villages telling the Gospel to God's "other sheep."

The summer was a dry one, and Thomas anxiously watched the dwindling creek from which his cattle and horses got their water supply. He had only one well and although it was a deep one, he feared it might not be sufficient if the creek should dry up.

"I'm going to dig another well," he announced one evening. "I've often thought there should be one out back of the barn. Sam Morgan thinks there's a vein of water coming down about there. He's good at judging such things. The corn is laid by now and the wheat cut. There isn't much to do until that second cutting of clover is ready. If we can get Dick Morgan to help us, we ought to be able to get a well dug by that time."

Sam Morgan came over, and with a twig of hazel in his hand walked back and forth across the lot, then designated the place where the well was to be.

"It turned so sharp there it almost twisted the bark off when I clutched it tighter," he said.

The well was begun. After they had dug so deeply that the dirt could no longer be tossed out, a windlass was erected by which it could be lifted out in buckets. While one man dug below, two of them manned the windlass. This was necessary lest some failure on the part of one man should allow the heavy bucket to reel back onto the digger. Usually Thomas did the digging. Whenever there was hard work to be done, he wanted to be in the midst of it. As Andrew and Dick turned the windlass they loved to sing some of the hymns they had learned at the conference. Hester, busying herself in house or chicken lot would smile softly and pray, "Dear Lord, keep them always this happy in whatever you have for them to do."

The well had gone down many feet. Thomas thought they would surely strike water soon. The boys were leaning against the ends of the windlass talking idly. Hester was looking anxiously at the cloudless sky and wishing it would rain so that she could have water to put on the ashes in the hopper. She was almost out of soap and she needed lye to make more. But it would take many bucketsful to soak the huge hopper of ashes and she dare not use it until the new well came in.

A faint call from below aroused the boys and Andrew leaned over to ask, "What is it, Father?"

"Send the bucket down. I have to come up. I'm sick."

Rapidly they lowered it, and when they saw Thomas safely astride the bucket they began to raise it, working with frantic speed. They did not say anything, but in each mind was the fearful thought, "damps," which every country boy early learned to dread. Thomas' head was near the top, and Dick braced himself to hold the weight while Andrew should lift his father. But before he could reach him total unconsciousness came. Thomas' hands loosened and, with Andrew clutching at the slackened rope, he fell back into the depths.

Hester heard the boys cry out and ran to their side. She did not need to be told what had happened. Andrew's gasp, "Dad! Damps!" was enough.

"I'm going down after him," Andrew said. "We can't wait for help. I'll bring him up. You help Dick man the windlass, Mother."

Before she could answer he was astride the bucket, and Hester threw her weight with Dick's against the windlass to prevent a too rapid descent. As they held they prayed. Well they knew that not only Thomas' life but Andrew's also was in grave danger. In a moment the slackened rope told them the bucket had touched bottom. Then came Andrew's voice.

"I've got him! Pull away!"

They did, frantically, and when Andrew's head appeared Hester put her whole weight against the pull while Dick dragged the men to safety. As they laid the unconscious man on the ground and Andrew had thrown himself in collapse beside him, Hester said, "Take your horse and go for the doctor, Dick. Go past Putneys and send Henry and one of the boys over. I'll take over here."

When Henry and his sons arrived, breathless from their half-mile run across the field and through the woods, Andrew was sitting up, looking pale but otherwise none the worse for his experience. His stay in the poisoned atmosphere had not been of sufficient duration to cause real damage.

Hester was coming around the corner of the chicken house dragging a heavy door. The men sprang to her assistance, and Henry said, "Good girl, Hester. That's the safest way to carry him."

They put the door down by Thomas' side, then slowly and carefully lifted him onto it. As they carried him through the doorway into the house Jim Putney said, "It's lucky this door isn't as wide as the doorway. We don't have to tilt it a bit."

And Hester, with one hand on Thomas' quiet wrist as she tried to take his pulse count, said calmly, "That's why I picked this door. Now we are going to put him down, door and all, on this bed and not move him again until the doctor comes."

["I know now where my dad got the calm strength that made him master of almost impossible circumstances," thought Dr. Andrew Lewis, seeming to see that whole scene now a century gone.]

For an hour longer they watched, Hester on one side, holding his hand, and Andrew standing motionless on the other. Outside, Henry Putney waited for the doctor and prayed for this friend who had been more than brother to him since childhood. When the sound of rapidly galloping hoofs told of the arrival of Dick and the doctor, he led the physician inside to the waiting group.

Thomas Lewis did not die, though he lay hovering between life and death for many days. The poison had been almost fatal and only a strong constitution could have thrown it off. Even when its effects had been overcome, there were other injuries that would take longer to heal. Five bones had been broken in his legs and ankles, and there was injury to the spine. The first few days had been filled with fear that the spinal cord might have been severed, for he lay motionless as the doctor set the bones and put on the splints. Hester knew sick dread then and had to reach through a blackness that her soul's eyes could not penetrate to find the Arm on which she must lean. She did find it, however, and it gave support when she had no strength of her own.

Through the long week until Thomas came back to painful consciousness they lived with the shadow of dread hanging over them. That fear was dispelled, however, when it was discovered that he could move his toes. Hester's heart grew light again. What did it matter if there *were* hard days and weary nights ahead of them if Thomas was to be restored whole to her again?

Then the thought of Andrew and his schooling came. He must not stay at home. She could run the farm alone. She could do the chores as well as Andrew any day! She could husk corn as rapidly as a man. It would be hard, but she could do it. And she would!

But Andrew had something to say on that subject. She tried to talk to him about it one evening when she waylaid him in the back lot out of earshot of the house. He would not listen to any of her plans.

"Listen to me instead, Mother. Of course I wanted to go to college. It was the biggest chance that ever came to me. But I wouldn't be worth a snap of anybody's finger there, knowing you were half killing yourself here. Dick and I have talked it over, and I know what I am going to do. I'm going to stay at home this year and keep things going on this farm. You couldn't do it and take care of Father, too. Why, even with me here we will have to have help with the corn husking."

Hester knew he was right but it was hard to see his plans for school discarded.

"But have we the right to keep you here? You are promised to the Lord's work, son."

"I promised to go wherever He wants me. I've done a lot of praying about this, Mother. I know He wants me here this year. You wouldn't have me go elsewhere, would you?"

"No," she said with a sob. "And He will bless you for the sacrifice, I know."

He put his arm around her shoulders, an unusual demonstration for the quiet lad, and spoke slowly, as if the change in his plans was still hard to discuss.

"Don't feel badly, Mother. Dick is going to buy a set of books for me—all that he has to get for himself. I'll study here at home. Father can probably help me a lot, and it will be good for him, too, to feel that he is helping. If I work hard maybe I can make up the lost time later. This is the way God is leading now, Mother, so let's not worry."

Thomas asked a few days later about when Andrew would be leaving, and had to be told that Dick had gone on without him. He groaned at the thought that his own incapacity should hinder his son's career, but Andrew would permit no morbid regrets.

"It's all right, Father. This is my place now. Let's not worry about the future. Whatever God has for me to do, He can make possible. Your job this year is going to be to make Greek and Philosophy, *et al*, a little less 'Greek' to me. Think you can do it?"

Thomas drew a long breath. "My Greek is rustier than an old nail, but give me time, and I'll try to polish it up. When do we start?"

Chapter Twenty-two

THE BOOKS CAME, and through the weeks when Thomas lay on his bed or sat in a chair with his lame legs propped on another chair in front of him, they worked on the lessons. It was not easy. Thomas' Greek, Latin, and mathematics were indeed rusty. He had been out of college more than twenty-five years, and the hard life of a farmer in a new country was not conducive to scholarly pursuits. Sometimes Henry Putney came over for a few hours, and the two friends tried together to resurrect the learning that had been buried under the accumulated acquirements of the years. They were chagrined to realize how much they had forgotten, but as the days went by, they began to enjoy the trip into the past.

Often Hester at her work would hear them laughing at the memory of some prank or joke that had been recalled through the books. It touched her deeply to note how eager Henry was to do anything he could to further Andrew's learning. She suspected that, had Henry been given the choice, he would have been proud to send his only daughter wherever the Lord might call.

If the learning came back slowly to the men, it was even more difficult for Andrew. After a day of corn husking in the cold air, he would be so tired that he would fall asleep over his books, and awaken later in shamefaced confusion. It was easier after the corn was in, for there were daytime hours that could be used for study. Dick came home at Christmas time, and the boys had a fine time comparing their learn-

147

ing. Andrew had made good progress in the languages and English, and Dick was sure that if the professors could hear the story and could realize the quality of the work he was doing at home, they would gladly permit him to enter as a second-year student the next year, and make up the necessary studies as he could.

That hope carried them through the winter. By spring Thomas was able to be about, at first on crutches, then with wo canes, and finally with only one. But all these exertions .eft his face drawn with pain. The broken bones had healed, but the injured back was still demanding its toll. He managed to help a bit about the chores, feeding the chickens, putting the grain in the feed boxes for the horses, or driving to the field with water for the men. But he could not stoop to gather the produce from the garden, nor could he lift a forkful of hay to the mangers.

Less and less as the summer advanced did they speak of Andrew's schooling, and when Dick went back in September, it was an accepted fact that Andrew could not go with him. Andrew's cheerful acceptance of the situation told his parents as no words could have done, that his surrender had been complete. All that he desired was his Master's will.

Still they hoped for complete recovery for Thomas. The doctor spoke of a specialist in St. Louis, that busy little city one hundred and fifty miles away on the Mississippi. But the trip overland would do more harm than Thomas could bear. The only water route was by way of the Wabash to the Ohio, thence to the Mississippi, and up to St. Louis. While smoother, it would be very slow and too great a risk.

"I heard the other day that they are planning to lay tracks into St. Louis and run cars drawn by a steam engine. That would be smooth going, I believe. But it will take a year or more to lay those tracks, and even then it may not come within a hundred miles of us."

"Do you think it will ever prove practical enough for real use?" questioned Thomas. "It would be a great thing for the inland places. We have to haul so far to market that we lose much of our profit. Will the railroads ever extend to the small places like this?"

"I don't know. It seems a very costly and dangerous thing to count on. As long as the rivers flow, the boat will be the main method of travel and commerce. That was the way the Maker intended. Man-made contraptions will never displace it."

As the months passed, the pain did not decrease. Hester wondered as she looked at Thomas whether his body or mind suffered most. The pain in his back became at times almost unendurable. But even worse was the knowledge to which they were all tacitly agreed, that Andrew could never leave the farm to seek a career of his own.

One night when Hester knew by the restless turning and twisting that Thomas was sleepless, she spoke to him.

"Is the pain bad, Thomas? Couldn't I help by rubbing?"

He groaned. "Rubbing won't help this pain, Hester. It is more than I thought I could ever stand, this knowing that because of my useless, cloddish old body, Andrew is tied here when he should be in school. I should think he'd hate me!"

"Why, Thomas Lewis! Don't let such thoughts stay in your mind one minute. He loves you so much he'd be glad to bear the pain himself if he could. I never saw a son more devoted to his father."

"Yes, I grant that. But he *should* hate me! I've ruined his career. If it weren't for me, he'd be in college now, preparing for the Lord's work. Now, thanks to me, he is just a farm hand."

"Father!" Andrew's voice spoke from the doorway. He was fully dressed at this past-midnight hour, and Hester knew, as must Thomas, that he had been out-of-doors wrestling with his problem rather than sleeping as a tired lad should. His voice went on with a new stern quality to it.

"Yes, just a farm hand! But a farm hand because that is where the Lord wants me. I wouldn't stay here even for you,

149

the best parents in the world, if I wasn't sure He wants me here."

"But He called you, my son!"

"Yes, He called me and I answered. He called me to yield and I answered, 'Anywhere, Lord.' I thought He was calling to the mission field—maybe it was because the preacher made it sound so alluring. But the promise I made to Him was that I'd go where He sent me. If He didn't send me, but just *held* me here, the promise is still good. It's because of His orders that I am here, not because of anything else!"

For a moment after he had finished his outburst, the room was in silence. Then there came a muffled sob as Thomas buried his face in his pillow. In a swift movement Andrew was across the floor. He knelt by the bed as Hester, on the other pillow, put a comforting arm across Thomas' shoulders. Andrew's long arm took both of them in.

"It's what I wanted to do," he said earnestly. "I don't want you to think I'm grudging Him this."

["He learned that word from his mother," thought Dr. Lewis.]

"I never did want to leave you, but I told Him I'd go wherever He said. He says, 'Right here at home,' and that's what it is to be. Can't we thank Him for it?"

They did, and from that day the tension was gone, and the old, happy atmosphere prevailed. Hester resumed her trips of mercy, and on the days when his back would permit, Thomas went with her.

Kate Putney came home from her long stay in the East. She was more beautiful than ever, and Sarah beamed with joy and pride. She brought back with her many new and novel ideas which she wanted to share with the other young people, and a round of parties followed. At first Andrew attended these, but more and more he found excuses for staying at home.

"Don't you like the gatherings the young folks have, son?" asked Hester one evening as he sat by the fireplace oiling a set of harness. She knew there was to be a party that night.

"Oh, they're all right, I guess."

"That doesn't sound as if you really thought so."

"Well—I like the games. They are fun. But they always wind up the evening with dancing, and I hate that! I'd feel like an ox clumping around over the floor, and I don't intend to put my arms around any girl's waist!"

Hester patted his shoulder in sympathy as Thomas smiled. "Some day you'll meet a girl you want to put your arms around," he said.

"I hope so. But till then I'll keep them where they belong."

"I don't think much of the dancing myself," Hester conceded. "But staying away makes you seem unfriendly."

"Some of the others are staying away, too. The first parties were fine, but lately—well, I don't like them."

The fact that Andrew had relinquished his plans for the mission field had at length been accepted by the community. Sarah and Hester began to dream again. Kate came back into the choir and was regular in church attendance. She and Andrew were friendly when they met, but there was no apparent effort to renew the former relationship.

One bright, sunny day in March when Hester and Thomas were looking through their packets of seeds saved from last year to decide just how to make this year's garden, and with Andrew stretched on the old "settle" reading *The Youth's Companion,* there came a clear whistle which they all recognized. Through the window they could see Kate on her horse. Andrew went out, then returned to say hastily, "I'm going for a ride with Kate."

They were gone for three hours. Where they went or what was said no one else ever knew. When Andrew came in at dusk after stabling his horse, he looked worn and troubled. Coming directly to stand before his parents, he spoke as if under compulsion.

"I want you two to know what happened this afternoon. No one else ever must know. Kate is going to tell her parents that she realizes that she has other ideas since being away and that we just wouldn't suit each other any more. But my parents have the right to know the truth. I hope you will understand. Kate didn't. She thinks I'm just being stubborn. She can't see that just the fact that I am going to stay at home doesn't make any difference at all. She still wouldn't be willing to go and be and do as the Lord led. I couldn't marry her without that. Do you see I couldn't?"

Hester's answer came slowly, while as usual Thomas waited. "Yes, we see. But I'm afraid it will make her feel very bad."

When Andrew spoke, his voice was thick with emotion.

"I didn't want to hurt her. I hope you believe that. It wasn't easy. She's still Katie. But she has changed in lots of ways, and she doesn't love the Lord as much as she loves Kate Putney. I couldn't do it."

This time it was Thomas who spoke. "We understand, son. We do understand."

In a few weeks Kate went East again, and that fall Sarah and Henry took the long stagecoach journey to see her married in her aunt's home. They came back with tales of the great plantation over which she would reign as mistress, and of the beauty and elegance of the wedding. But in Sarah's eyes there was desolation. Her boys were still with her, but Katie, her darling, was gone.

The next year Andrew brought home his bride, little Ruthie Barnes who had stood by his side at that altar of consecration years ago. She had spent those years caring for her father and her younger brothers and sisters. Now a stepmother had come into the home, and she was free to take the next step of the Lord's leading.

Hester and Thomas had wondered if Andrew would ever love another woman as he had loved Kate. But when they saw the look he gave Ruthie as he helped her from the buggy, they were reassured. Never had Andrew given Kate the kind of love he was giving Ruthie. He had found the one woman God had planned for him.

Chapter Twenty-three

THERE WAS LITTLE WRITTEN in the diary during the next few years. Perhaps life was flowing in such a smooth, undisturbed stream that there was little to record. Andrew's and Ruth's children, Tom, Mary, and Benjy, came and filled their grandparents' lives with interest and joy. Another house was built, one that Andrew said would be strong and beautiful after one hundred years.

["It is," thought the other Andrew Lewis. "Sid wishes it weren't quite so well built. Getting through those walls with water pipes hasn't been a joke."]

It stood closer to the road than the old house did, and on the day that Benjy was born Andrew planted six elm trees on the lawn. When Hester held this tiny baby in her arms and heard the name that had been given him, she felt a solemn joy to realize God had sent this mite to fill the place that had been empty in her heart since that tragic spring flood fifteen years before.

"He's such a tiny thing, Thomas. Less than five pounds on my butter scales. It will take a lot of care and love to make a big boy of him."

"You are able to supply both, Hettie girl. If the love and care he gets are to be the measure of his size, he will be as large as Goliath."

She sat for a long time looking down into the face of the baby. When she looked up, her eyes had a faraway look as if she saw things above and beyond the farm kitchen where she sat.

"Thomas, it frightens me! This little fellow is just starting out on the long road that will be his life. I love him so much that I feel that I must go with him to watch over every step and see that his little feet don't go astray. But I'll never be able to do it. I'm almost an old woman now, and I'll be gone before he grows up!"

Thomas laughed. "What do you call old, Hettie? If I can figure rightly, you aren't fifty yet. Do you call that old?"

"Yes, when I compare it with this little fellow's age. Why, when he is as old as I am now——"

"You and I will be with our Lord. That same Lord can take care of little Benjy, Grandma. Let's leave it with Him."

She said no more, but that night she wrote in her diary:

> The road ahead looks so long and rough for those little feet. I must hunt through my Bible to find the words of assurance I need. I know they are there. God would not leave us to wonder when it is the soul safety of our little ones that concerns us.

She did find them, and often in the following pages she would write down those promises. There were many, and she hungrily fed on them. Often she would read them to Thomas as they sat together at the close of the day. Then, having gained the assurance she needed for little Benjy, her far-seeing eyes looked beyond him and saw other forms traveling down that same long road.

"I can't see the end, Thomas. The road goes on and on, farther than my eyes can see. Benjy will grow old, too, and his children and grandchildren will need guidance and help. There are bound to be temptations to turn them from the way. I can't see that the world is getting one bit better for all the learning we have and the improvements that are made. I yearn over those children to come. I can't stand it to think that some of them might miss the way. I feel responsible for them."

"Pshaw, Hettie! God won't hold you responsible for children born long after you're dead."

"How do you know He won't? If I raised Andrew rightly, he will do the same by his children, and they by theirs. But mistakes could be passed on."

"Sure. And they could marry someone who hadn't had the right bringing up. You can't run other folks lives after you're dead, Hettie. Better be satisfied with bossing me around down here, and let it go at that."

"Quit your joking, Thomas. This isn't funny. They'll all be my descendants, won't they? And just as they may inherit my physical traits, so they may get my weaknesses. And I'll be responsible!"

"Not forever, you won't be. I'm sure there is a point at which all relationship with you will cease, where every trace of your blood will have disappeared from their bodies. I know there's a legal limit to the relationship. I can show you that in the old law books on the shelf."

"But a *man* or a bunch of men wrote those books. They can't tell how God will figure. I *am* responsible to those future generations, Thomas Lewis, and so are you. If we hadn't loved and married and had our children, those people that will live and love and have families a hundred, maybe five hundred years from now, would never exist. That's a terrifying thought. If I had realized that when I was sixteen years old, I wonder if I would have had the courage to marry."

"I'm glad you didn't, then. Having awakened to the fact, just what are you going to do about it now?"

"I am going to my Bible, and I am going to see if I can find some ground on which to take a stand in believing that if I trust in the Lord, I can be assured that not one of those who live, or will live, because of me shall ever depart from the road of life."

Evening after evening she pored over her Bible and the concordance that had been a gift from Thomas on their thirtieth wedding anniversary. She found so many verses to delight her that he had to get pen and paper and make a list. Again

155

and again she would interrupt Thomas' reading to share her discoveries.

"Listen to this: 'Oh, that there were such a heart in them that they would fear me, and keep all my commandments always, that it might be well with them and with their children forever.' Doesn't that show that God holds each generation responsible for those that come after? He says 'their children forever.' Don't you think that when God says 'forever' He means that?"

"Rather guess He does."

"Here's another verse from the same chapter. 'These words which I command thee this day shall be in thine heart; and thou shalt teach them diligently unto thy children and shalt talk of them when thou sittest in thine house and when thou walkest by the way, and when thou liest down, and when thou risest up.' That's how He wants us to teach our children about Him. That's how we can make it well with them forever."

"You're all right, Hettie. Just keep on seeking. You may yet convince your skeptical old husband."

Other verses there were to which she turned often: "The children of thy servants shall continue, and their seed shall be established before thee." And, "The mercy of the Lord is from everlasting to everlasting upon them that fear him, and his righteousness unto children's children."

But the verses that seemed to satisfy her as the complete answer to her need, were the assurances of answered prayer.

" 'If ye abide in me and my words abide in you, ye shall ask what you will and it shall be done unto you.' That's a limitless promise, Thomas, but it hangs on a condition that I have to fulfill. It's one I've been trying to live up to for many years. I'm not saying I've always lived so entirely for Him as I should, but I do believe I abide in Him. I couldn't have taken life if I didn't. And more and more as I study and read, His words abide in me. Do you think He will let me claim that verse?"

"I think He will, Hettie girl," answered Thomas huskily.

"And here's another I *know* I can claim. 'All things whatsoever ye ask in prayer, believing, ye shall receive.' Oh, I do believe! I know! And He said '*all* things,' and ye 'shall' receive. I'm just, right now, taking my stand there. It pleasures me more than anything I ever had happen to me to know I can do that."

Thomas reached out a hand to lovingly smooth the dark hair. In spite of the more than thirty years that had passed, she was still like the starry-eyed girl he had brought over the mountains.

Thomas and Hester stayed on in the log house after the new one was built. It was home to them, the home which had seen the births of their children and which had echoed to their shouts and play, the home from which all those children had gone forth, one to a home of his own and the others to the Father's Home above. They did not want to leave it although Andrew and Ruth would have welcomed them to the other house.

The farm prospered in those years. Andrew had to hire two and sometimes three "hands" during the cropping season. Thomas had revived the knowledge of basketry learned from Hester during that first winter, and was selling his baskets as fast as he could make them. He had worked out new and beautiful designs for the fancy baskets, and people came for many miles to buy them.

He was still helping the people "up the creek," or at Hickory Center, as it was now called. He could not go to them as much as formerly, so they came to him. Whenever a man had to go past the farm on his way to the village, he was apt to drop in for a chat. These chats often lasted for an hour or more as the man unburdened his heart of his problems. Oftentimes these problems concerned others, some dispute over a stray hog or some unpaid debt. These men were wary and suspicious of the lawyers in town. Thomas found that often he could get the differing parties together and, with a bit of friendly counsel, clear up the differences.

He took down the old law books and spent many hours reading them, finding in the cases cited there a precedent for the settling of some trouble in this day. Andrew liked to tease him by calling him "Lawyer Lewis" or "Squire," but Thomas went on in his kindly ministry. He accepted no fees for his services, for he assured them that he was only dealing in friendship. But as the years passed, the Center lost its unsavory reputation, and to the dwellers there, if not to the outside world, the credit belonged to Thomas and Hester Lewis.

Thomas had another interest that was a source of great satisfaction to him and pride to Hester. With the more frequent mail service that the recent years had brought, he subscribed to several newspapers and magazines. Once, in rebuttal of an article which gave a distorted view of western life, he had written and sent in his own appraisal of affairs in the Illinois country. It brought enthusiastic response, and a check for five dollars, also a request for more. So he regularly wrote of the conditions around him and of the lives of his neighbors, giving, in a graphic style which he had not known he possessed, a picture of the growth of the young state. The check that came monthly was put aside as an "over and above" gift to the Lord. Andrew, they knew, was paying a full half of Dick Morgan's support as he labored in India, and they rejoiced to have this extra bit to add to their own regular gifts.

Chapter Twenty-four

FOR A LONG TIME there had been ominous rumblings from Washington which presaged trouble of a serious nature between the slave and free states. There had been rioting and bloodshed around St. Louis over the activities of the abolitionist printer, Elijah Lovejoy. From other places came rumors of bitter differences. But the dwellers in the little valley paid small heed to them. Their lives were full of work, and they had no time to give to speculation as to what might happen.

Thomas alone, having more time to read, seemed to sense the import of it all. When Lincoln was elected, he predicted trouble, and when Fort Sumter fell, it only came as the confirmation of his fears. A volunteer company was organized in the village. Both Will and Jim Putney, married now and having young families, went, over the protests of their wives and the hysterical pleading of Sarah. Andrew came home from the meeting in the square with a sobered look on his face. He had offered himself, wondering what would happen to his family but feeling that he must go. But the captain of militia under whom he had tried to enlist, had talked him out of it.

"I know you feel like you ought to go, Andrew. All of us do. But somebody has to stay at home and get this year's crops in. You have two families to think of, too."

"But Bill and Jim Putney are in and they have families."

"Yep. And their dad is still supportin' the hull of them.

159

We couldn't make them Putney boys stay home if we tied 'em. They think it's goin' to be a big lot of fun. Did you ever know a Putney not to want to be in on the fun? Go on home, Andrew. It will be all over in three months, and you need to get your crops in."

So he had come home to again subordinate his own choice to that of his Leader. Later when they began to draft young men, he was again passed by. His response to this was an increased effort on the farm. Feeling as if it were his part of the war, he worked early and late to wrest from the soil the greatest amount of food possible for man and beast. He grew more silent, but more tender. By this only did Hester know that he felt pain at not being at the front.

Kate came home on a visit, and Hester was shocked at the change in her. Her former gaiety had been replaced by petulance. Her sweet smile that had been her chief charm was gone and in its place was a perpetual pout. It was hard to see in this spoiled woman the little girl that had played at housekeeping with Mary around the roots of the maple tree. Once Hester caught her watching Andrew and Ruth as they stood together at church, and the jealousy in her face was so plain that Hester was shamed for her. She looked to see if Andrew had noticed it, but his eyes were upon Ruth as she spoke to him, and Hester thought thankfully, "It's all right. Andrew has eyes for only one woman and that's Ruthie."

Kate quarreled with her youngest brother, Harry, while she was at home. Harry was much disgruntled and unhappy because he had not been allowed to go with his older brothers. The father, sick at heart over Sarah's grief for the other boys, had sternly forbidden the lad to go.

"You can't do that to your mother, boy. She has enough to bear now. Don't give her any more to grieve over. Anyway, I need you here. It'll be all we can do to keep things going this summer without the other boys, and you can't hire help for love or money. The boys will probably be back in time for corn husking, but somebody's got to run this farm till then."

Harry yielded, but he was surly and ill-tempered, and when Kate was telling one day of the magnificence and luxury of life on their plantation, Harry burst out.

"Yeah! But what will it be like when Lincoln and our soldiers turn all those slaves loose? You gonna pick tobacco worms?"

"Shut up, Harry Putney! You don't know what you're talking about. Nobody'd *dare* free our slaves. They're *ours*!"

"Just you wait and see!" he taunted.

The mother, hearing the altercation, came in to find them in furious battle, the angry words flying hot and fast. She managed to quiet them but the wound did not heal. When Kate left two weeks later, Harry had not spoken to her again. She on her part was indignant and frightened at what life had brought and what the future might hold. Hester, trying to comfort Sarah later, thought sadly, "He that findeth his life shall lose it."

The boys did not come back in three months. The news from the front was alarming. More volunteers were called for, and reports came in of staggering losses in battle. Thomas said sadly, "Can this be our country in such a war between brothers?"

The months grew into years. Jim Putney was sent home with a wound that would prevent his return. Bill was reported missing, and they could not discover if he were dead or in a southern prison. Harry grew more restless and resentful. At last he was called in the draft, and rejoiced openly at his "good luck." Sarah was frantic. Henry was stern, feeling that now Sarah must let the lad go.

"I can't," she moaned. "He's my baby, Henry. Do something!"

"There's nothing to do. Our boy is no better than—than Jed Barlow's boy. He has already gone. Ours will have to."

"No he won't!" she said stubbornly. "He shan't! You've got money, Henry. What's it good for if it can't protect our boy now?"

"We can't do that Sarah."

"Well, if you can't, I can. I've got some money, don't you forget. And I'll find somebody who needs that money and will go in Harry's place. I will, I tell you!"

Hester never knew how it was accomplished, but when the next contingent left from the village, Harry was not among them. A substitute had been found. Andrew heard later that Wes Collins from one of the little farms back in the hills had desperately needed money for a mortgage payment and had "sold himself," as Andrew put it, to save Harry Putney. No one knew how the boy himself took it, but Hester's heart ached for him. She knew he would feel it a disgrace to be so bought off while his brothers and others had gone and were paying the price in blood. He did not go any place, and would not talk about it even to his father.

Six months later, after word had come that Wes Collins had died in battle, Andrew came in one evening to report gravely, "Maybe you'd better go over to Putney's, Mother. Harry has run away and they are sure he has gone to war. Aunt Sarah is wild!"

"How did he manage that?"

"Nobody knows. But it's a good guess that is what he did."

"The poor boy! He probably thinks he should go in Wes Collins' place. I'll go and do what I can, but the words will be hard to find. Sarah has lived to see that she who saveth her child shall lose him, to paraphrase the Scripture a bit."

"I know it. This isn't the first time either," he said soberly.

There seemed no comfort for Sarah. She had lost her son more truly than if he had fallen in battle. The war ended, the other boys came home. But Bill Putney's name was among those who died in Andersonville, and Harry was not heard from. Bill's wife and little girl lived with her people. Jim helped Henry on the farm and lived in a house across the field from the big house which was now so silent. Jim's little girls were quiet, colorless children, lacking completely the sparkle that had distinguished the other Putneys. Henry sadly commented that, having had three strong sons, he felt cheated to have no grandsons.

Kate's husband had returned from the war with one leg gone and his face terribly scarred. They were living in poverty on the plantation that was now a scene of desolation and ruin. Kate's letters home were filled with bitterness. The wealth that had been her pride was gone. She had nothing left that could compensate. She resented having to do the work of the household while her husband struggled with the land. She would not come home. She was in no mood to face those who, in her opinion, had helped to ruin them. So the years passed and Time, the great healer, began to cover the wounds.

Chapter Twenty-five

THE LOW LAND of southern Illinois had always been miasmic, but as farms had been drained the condition had improved. For some years the scourge of malaria had seemed to be on the retreat. But the year that young Tom, Andrew's oldest son, was fifteen, was an unusually wet one. The water rose from the creeks and overflowed the lowlands. When the streams subsided, they left large areas covered with water that had no outlet. The humid atmosphere did not hasten evaporation. The mosquitos came in swarms and made life an agony. From every mudhole and stagnant pool they flew in clouds. When had there ever been such a time? Hester wondered if Pharaoh and his Egyptians had suffered a worse plague.

When several of the villagers fell ill, no one wondered. This was just the kind of year for malaria to raise its ugly head. But the disease did not follow the regular course, and before long the dread word "typhoid" passed from lip to lip. Soon reports of widespread illness came from other parts of the country, and the epidemic raged.

Jim Putney was the first in the community to go, and Sarah was desolate indeed. Of the merry group of boys that had romped over the farm, not one was left to her. Even her daughter was too far away to come to her. Then Jim's wife and one little girl were taken. Henry went home from their funeral to take to his own bed with a chill and headache, and two weeks later he, too, was gone. The disease seemed to strike hardest at the strong men, although in many homes every member would be stricken. The death rate was over fifty per cent of those stricken. Hester was busy day and night, caring for the ill, comforting the bereaved, and preparing the dead for burial. Thomas worried about her, but she reassured him.

"I won't suffer. The Lord surely wants someone to do this work, and I'm better able than most. He will care for me."

She herself felt some concern about Andrew, for he was working too hard, trying to do his own work and that on the Putney farm also. But she did not think that Thomas, who kept closely at home, would be endangered. So it struck her with almost paralyzing shock when she returned from a neighbor's home one evening to find him ill. All too well she knew the symptoms and had on hand the remedies that could be administered while awaiting the doctor. Day and night she was at his side, but after the first week, he did not know her. At the end of the third week, on that fateful "twenty-first day" that brought the crisis, she heard the last labored breath, and gently closed the eyes that would not smile on her again until they met in a better land. Sarah and Andrew did all that was to be done, just as Hester and Andrew had cared for the mortal remains of Henry Putney a few weeks before.

Andrew and Ruth begged her to stay with them that night. But she wanted to be alone in her own home. So, in the place where they had dwelt together, she kept her vigil, and came forth the next day to face the years ahead. In that long night she had been on a mountaintop and had seen her transfigured Lord in all His glory. She had fallen on her face in complete abandonment to Him. Now she had come down to live and serve among men until that Lord should come for her. She was not defeated, but she was stripped of the things of earth that might hinder her vision. From henceforth she would see "no man save Jesus only."

The cemetery by the church had to be enlarged, and Sarah Putney gave another acre of land for that purpose. The preacher could not keep up with the demands on him, and several times Hester Lewis stood by the graveside in his stead and spoke the last words of committal. And there came a day when, with Ruthie and the three fatherless children, she saw Andrew laid to rest with the other children who had gone on so long ago. Before they turned away to go back to the lonely home, she lifted her eyes and murmured, "The children are all in. Thank You, Father."

By the time winter came, the epidemic was broken. New wells were dug and the old ones filled in. The doctors advised that covers be kept on the wells so that the mosquitoes might not reach the water, and that all new wells be dug at a distance from the outbuildings. All over the land prayers were sent up that never again would such a scourge be sent upon them.

["The lessons learned then are still being used," commented Dr. Lewis. "I studied about that epidemic. It was the spark that set off the battle against typhoid. That battle went on for generations, but it's practically won now."]

The scars of that awful summer would remain as long as those who had been through it lived. In the "new house" Ruthie faced life courageously. Young Tom, like his father before him, gave up dreams of an education and bent his shoulders to the yoke. Even Mary and Benjy could help, and somehow they managed.

In the house across the creek, the big colonial mansion that Sarah Putney had planned with so much anticipation, she sat with only Jim's little Polly to keep her company. Katie could not come to her mother as her husband lay ill and needed her. Help was almost impossible to obtain. Should she sell the farm that she and Henry had developed and move into the village? Her heart cried out against it, but what else could she do? The day that Hester drove past and saw Sarah cutting corn in the field while little seven-year-old Polly drove the team, her heart was shocked and grieved. Sarah, who had not worked in the fields for forty years!

The morning after this as she sat at her table eating breakfast and pondering on what she could do to help her old friend, there came a knock on her door. She faced the man who stood on her step with no consciousness of having seen him before. It was only when he spoke falteringly that she recognized him.

"Do you know me, Aunt Hettie?"

"Harry Putney! Oh, you dear boy!"

She had her arms around him and drew him inside. It was as if one had risen fom the dead. What joy to have one of the boys left! She made him sit down and eat with her. He was trembling with nervousness and emotion, and the hot coffee was just what he needed. She did not ply him with questions but waited until he was ready to speak. At last he reached across the table and put his strong young hand over her roughened one.

"Bless you, Aunt Hettie! You always were good to me. I don't think I could have come back if I hadn't heard you were still here."

"Where have you been?"

"Not far away. You know why I had to go, don't you? I couldn't stay here another day with Bill gone, Jim crippled, and Wes Collins dead in my place. I just couldn't! So I left. It doesn't matter now how I managed it, but I did. I got into the war. There wasn't much time left, but I did see some fighting and I was wounded at Five Forks. I felt better after that, as if I had paid a part of my debt. I had a bad time, but I got well and am none the worse for the experience. But I had another job yet to do. Wes Collins had a wife and baby some place and I had to care for them. I sneaked back to the hills where he had lived, and learned they had gone back to her folks in Kentucky. So I followed her and told her I was going to help her."

He stopped for a minute, then gave an embarrassed laugh.

"She's an awfully sweet girl, Aunt Hettie. We've been married three years and now we have two little boys. I feel pretty lucky to have so much."

167

"God has been good to you, Harry. I wish your father could have known it."

"So do I. But it was only last week that I heard what had happened here. A fellow who used to live on the other side of the village went past Lecie's brother's house and told him. It made me realize how selfish I've been. You've had a sad time too, Aunt Hettie. I'm sorry."

"Yes, it was a sad time. But I've still got Ruthie and the children, and there's always work to do. It's all right, Harry. I'm not grudging them to the Lord. He gave, and in the right time He took away. Blessed be His name."

Harry sat silent for a minute, then said anxiously, with a note of doubt in his voice, "My mother? Will she see me?"

"Do you come in love, Harry?"

"Oh yes! I want to—well, there's nobody to take care of her now, and Lecie and I want to do it. Will you go with me to see her, Aunt Hettie?"

Together they rode up to the lonely house and found Sarah with a big shawl wrapped about her, standing on her porch looking toward the church on the hill and the pine grove beside it. She faced them inquiringly, and Hester wondered what she should say. But she had no chance to say anything. Sarah took one look and opened her arms.

Hester rode back alone. She was glad that the horse knew the way, for she could not see for the mist in her eyes. Sarah would yet have joy in her family. And the name of Putney would not die. Sarah, as well as Harry, had learned a lesson.

"She won't have seven more sons and three more daughters like Job did, but the God of Job will bless her, I'm sure."

["Harry Putney! That must be Kay's ancestor," said Andy Lewis. "The name surely didn't die. There's dozens of them about."]

Chapter Twenty-six

LIFE WAS STILL FULL and rich for Hester Lewis. She kept up her visits to the backwoods homes. She helped the doctors bring babies into the world. She counseled with the discouraged mothers about better care for them. She taught in the home Sunday school on Sunday mornings, then rode horseback to the hill school that was her pride.

She and Ruthie managed the farm together. They kept young Tom in school until he had finished the academy. He was large and strong and was soon able to fill a man's place in the fields. Hester watched him fondly and saw him grow daily more like his father. Her memory was still keen, but her tongue would betray her, and often she called him Andrew.

She saw Mary grow into lovely womanhood and eventually leave them to go to India with Hugh Morgan, Dick's oldest son. The day she left them, Hester, with eyes filled with the tears the parting brought forth, felt her heart swell with joy and pride. At last Andrew was going to the mission field in the person of his daughter. Hester lived to see Mary's children follow in her footsteps.

She saw Benjy yearning for the training he did not have the heart to ask for, and she shared with Ruthie and Tom the eight years of sacrifice that sent him into the world equipped for a surgeon's career. Nor did she count it a waste when he lost his life ministering to the soldiers during the Indian wars.

She saw Tom's children grow up around her. When the

first one, her great-grandson, was laid in her arms, and she saw a tiny deformed foot, she held him closely.

"Oh, you precious baby!" she whispered, "I wish I could make the little foot right. You're so little and so weak, and the way ahead is so long and hard. I'd like to travel it for you, and save you all the bumps of it. But I can't. I'm an old lady now, and surely I'll reach the end of my journey soon. I'd like to give you something to take along to strengthen you for the fight, my little Andrew, but I can only give you my love, and pray that God will bless and keep you."

She laid him back in the cradle. It seemed too hard to be borne that she must pass on and would not be here to help this crippled mite over the rough places.

"Oh, God, be with him!" she prayed. "I guess I've been too sure of my own strength and haven't trusted enough to You. For the first time I'm realizing that I can't always be here to help those I love. I've known it before, but now I'm *feeling* it. Dear God, be with not only this little fellow, but with all the others that will come along the road behind him—his children and his children's children, through all the generations that will come before our Lord comes back. It would be more than I could bear if I did not believe You were sufficient to keep them all. Be with each one, Lord. That's the only gift I can give them that will last. I give them You!"

Hester lived many years after that, and when she was ninety-five years old she sat in her old rocker while that crippled great-grandson laid in her arms his own little son.

"His name is Thomas, Grandmother. Thomas III. And maybe he can go to the Congo in place of the others of us who couldn't go. He is strong and straight. No board will turn *him* down."

"He will go where God sends," she answered in a voice that quavered with age and emotion. "You, Tom, like my son Andrew, gave up your own plans to serve Him where He set you. And young Andrew here has given himself to whatever service was asked in spite of his handicap. God will enable this little Thomas, as He has enabled all of you, to answer His call and serve Him selflessly, whatever the price may be. Take him now, Andrew—I'm very tired."

There was only one more entry in the diary. In wavering letters Hester had written for the last time.

"I am almost at the end of my journey. It has been a long road and a hard one at times. And for many years it has been a very lonely one. But the Lord has always borne the heavy end of the load. And in the lonely hours He came to company with me. Now I will soon be taken to meet my dear Thomas and our children. I will be *so* happy to see them.

"But the road winds on. And the line of the Lewis family goes on also. And my heart yearns over the boys and girls that will become the men and women of the future. Oh, dear God, be with them. Just one thing I am asking for them, and I'm thanking You now for the promise that assures it. May they all be Thine, Lord, and may every one of them travel in the way You lead and be profitable to You.

"And if, in the long years ahead, Father, one of them should falter in his appointed task and seek to turn aside from the way of Thy choosing, oh, be with him and send some messenger to draw him back to Thee. When the enemy comes in like a flood, raise up Thy standard before him. That's all I can do, Father—just commit them to Thy care, until Jesus comes!"

Beneath this was written by another hand:

Hester Field Lewis went to be with the Lord
September 10, 1900.
Aged 95 years, 1 month and 16 days.

BOOK III

Chapter Twenty-seven

D R. ANDREW LEWIS CLOSED THE BOOK. How long he had been reading he did not, for the moment, remember. He looked about him at the room; some of the furnishings were older than the cabin. He seemed to be living in the days when the brave and noble ones whom he had met in the old book still lived and labored here. It would not have seemed incongruous should the door have opened to admit Hester Lewis just returned from one of her trips of mercy.

He went to the back door and looked out. Just so must Hester have stood many times, facing the hills across the creek. Men may change, but the hills remain. She must have seen, on the mornings when she arose in the darkness to begin the long day's toil, the dawn begin to color the sky just as it was doing now.

From near at hand came the scent of nasturtiums, their spicy fragrance intensified by the dew. Andy had thought that odd V-shaped arrangement a rather unique idea for a flower bed. Now he realized that the queer bulk was all that was left of Hester's lye hopper where she obtained the lye for her soap-making. Hester and Thomas Lewis had passed from the earth, yet these material things they had handled remained. Did something else remain, also? Had they left a heritage of faith and endurance and self-sacrifice that would pass on from parents to children as they, too, traveled the long road? His father had been that last small baby that she had cradled in her feeble arms and breathed a prayer over.

175

"That baby did get to the Congo, Grandma Hester," he whispered. "He gave the Congo his life."

Somehow the thoughts of the Congo did not hurt as they had. In the quiet of this dawn, which reminded him of the breathless dawns of the African jungle, all the old bitterness and pain had vanished. The sorrows and heartaches which had seemed too great to be borne faded into insignificance in the long view that the old diary had given him. In that book he had lived with those earlier Lewises through all the varying years of their lives, through the shifting sunshine and shadow that make up living. And he had seen how sorrow, disaster, and even death softened with the passage of time and became the shading that brought out the beauty of the picture. He had learned how, through almost a century, one woman had walked with God. Like Caleb, she had "wholly followed the Lord," and God had heard and answered her prayers by sending, in the time that had passed since then, His messengers to guide and safeguard her descendants that not one of them should lose his way.

In his own soul where for weeks there had been storm there was now perfect peace. He did not know what the future held for him nor where the path led—to the Congo with its dirt and disease and darkness and its glorious opportunity for service, or to a consecrated ministry of healing in this land with Kay to go with him down the long road. Of only one thing he was sure, his future rested in the all-wise, all-loving hand of his Father. All he had to do was to wait in stillness of soul until the Father was ready to reveal His will.

The faint glow in the East had become bright with the promise of a new day. The fowls in their coops were stirring and the animals in the lot were moving restlessly. From the trees by the lane came the wakening chirps of the birds getting ready to greet the daybreak. Grandpa came limping across the yard, his face brightening as he saw Andy up and dressed.

"Andy boy, you up a'ready?"

"Yes, I didn't sleep well. What about you?"

"I didn't sleep so well either. Wasn't much breeze up in my room."

"Tell you what, Grandpa. Let's leave a note for Sid, and take the car and run up to the hilltop where we can see the sunrise better. We can get back in time to get breakfast for Sid by the time he is ready."

The old man's face lighted. "That would be great. I did that once or twice in my life when I lived here. But usually there were too many things to be done even at daybreak. If I got up early, so did the cows, and then the day's work just reached out and grabbed me."

Andy drove slowly that they might enjoy the scents of the dew-wet grasses and weeds along the roadway. When they came out on the hilltop, the whole horizon lay before them in a blaze of pink and gold and gray. They watched as the sun slipped up over the edge until it became a full disk.

"It's a new day," said Andy reverently. "Grandpa, before we go down to face what it has for us, won't you pray?"

Grandpa's voice was husky, but there was a ring of joy in it as he thanked God for all that the past had brought them and asked His blessing on the future.

They drove back down the hill in silence except for Andy's soft whistling. Grandpa did not recognize the tune. It sounded like a hymn, but it was one he had never heard, a most poignant, haunting one. Sometime he must ask Andy what it was. Just now he wanted only to listen in stillness.

Grandpa had been heavy of heart these last weeks, not because of the death of his son, for he had given that son to God before he was born, and was not "grudging" that gift now, as Grandmother Hester would have said. But he had known there was bitter struggle going on in his grandson's soul. It would be tragedy, in Grandpa's opinion, if something should happen to keep Andy from stepping into that empty place on the Congo field. Andy had given no confidences, and Grandpa had asked none. He had only prayed. The answer had come. What the fight had been about, he would probably never know.

177

But he did know that last night had in some manner brought the victory. He felt that soon as he ate a bite of breakfast, he could lie down on the davenport and get some real sleep!

Andy went about his tasks that morning with a whistle on his lips. Sid listening to him, smiled.

"That sounds better. More like the old Doc should. I haven't known what to say to him, but I've felt that he was mighty low. It *has* been hard with Uncle Tom dying just at this time. And with Kay away he's been extra lonesome. I *know*. Don't think I'll ever let Grace go off this way again. Listen to that whistle, will you! Now if he'd just start some of his bird calls and the birds begin to answer, I'd know he was okay."

Andy did not start the bird calls, however. He just kept up the soft whistling that had an almost solemn sound to it, and at last Sid recognized it, and rejoiced at its message.

> Master, the terror is over,
> The elements sweetly rest.
> My soul in the calm lake is mirrored
> And heaven's within my breast.
> Whether the wrath of the storm-tossed sea,
> Or demons or men or whatever it be,
> They all shall sweetly obey Thy will,
> Peace, peace be still!

In midmorning, after Grandpa had lain down for his nap and Sid had again refused his offer of help, Andy said, "I've prepared everything for dinner so that you can get it in a very short time, Sid. Will it inconvenience you much if I'm away today?"

"Go ahead, Doc. You've been a mighty good scout to help me out the way you have. I'm on the last lap now. Everything will be shipshape when Grace comes home Saturday. Go have yourself a time of some sort."

Andy laughed. "I'm not going on a spree. You needn't worry. I just want a day in the open before we go back.

Tell Grandpa when he wakes up that I have a lunch and will be back for supper."

He stopped at the corner to get his mail, then drove on into the hills. To the highest one he went, the one where he and Kay had stopped together on that day many weeks ago. Half whimsically he thought that if he were to get any revelation as to God's will for him, a mountaintop would be an appropriate place to receive it.

He had hoped, as he did each day, that there would be a letter from Kay, and as usual, he had been disappointed. This time he realized that perhaps it were better so. When he had decided on his own course, it would be time enough to talk to her. Perhaps it was God's hand that had restrained her from writing until he should know where his course lay.

He opened the only letter that had come. It was a thick one from Roy Allison. It had been sent to his room in the city, then forwarded to Uncle Charlie's house, then here. It was the first direct word he had heard from the Congo since his father's death, and he read it eagerly.

Dear Andy:

I know you will want to hear all about your father. I will do my best to tell you, but it is still hard for me to realize it is true, although I have only to look from my window to see that fresh grave with its bank of all the flowers we could procure. Just two days ago he performed a very difficult operation, and the nurses were all telling of his speed and efficiency. None of us dreamed he was not well. Maybe he pushed himself too hard that day—maybe he just was called to pay in one big lump sum the cost of the overwork he has done for years. It is a calculated risk we all take, but we know it is worth it. If your father could speak to us now, he would say the same—it is worth the cost. He just went to sleep, Andy, and never wakened. The poor heart was too tired.

One thing had disturbed him greatly. The fetish worshipers have been bad this year. A new cult has been introduced from the South. Its followers have not only led hosts of the people off into their devilish beliefs, but they are mixing in politics in the cities, and the young folks who have gone in there to work are returning to stir up strife and revolution. David has been seen a great deal in the company of one of the leaders but, knowing the boy's zeal for souls, we all thought he was witnessing to him. It never dawned on us that David might be attracted by such a thing. We all thought him solidly established. Now we don't know what to think. Four days ago, just two days before your father died, David disappeared. He was last seen going off into the jungle with this cult leader. The fellow had a lot of his hideous paraphernalia with him, and a crowd of his followers were tagging along behind, as if they were going out to perform some of their awful ceremonies. David was not being forced to go. He was laughing and chatting with the leader. It seemed that he was one of them. However, we did not really worry until the night passed and he did not return. Never before had he gone for even a few hours without telling your father where he would be. Next day some of those followers came straggling back. When asked about David, they all tell the same story, that he had gone on a trip with the leader, probably to Leopoldville.

One of two things is true. Either he is voluntarily living with them and has become one of them, or he is being held against his will. If that latter is true, we will eventually hear from him unless he has been killed. Somehow, I don't think they'd dare do that. In any case, it was agony for your father. We all loved David as a brother, and he was as a son to your dad. He felt as he would have felt if you had gone under those circumstances.

We laid our dear doctor to rest beside your mother and the children. Just two weeks ago David had cut the grass, trimmed the vines and made a graveled walk in the little "God's Acre" where our loved ones lie. He said he wanted it to be nice when you get here.

We are all eagerly awaiting your arrival with the little lady whose picture stands by yours on your father's desk. It will be a sad homecoming for you, but we will all do our best to soften the loss we know you feel. You will not need to be told how desperately you are needed at the hospital.

We are all praying for David and will let you know if we get any knowledge of him. Love from all of us,

Roy Allison

Andy laid the letter aside and threw himself down in the grass under the tree. With his head pillowed on his arms he lay, feeling the warm breeze as a soothing touch. He was relaxed as he had not been since Kay's letter came on that day that now seemed months ago. He had a sense of God's nearness, and knew that he could now listen to the Spirit's voice unhindered by his grief over either his father or Kay. He saw things in the right perspective at last. He realized that all his former plans had been made without consulting the Lord.

He had been directed and controlled by his love for his father. From earliest childhood his supreme desire had been to please his dad. Seeing the other's devotion to his work and to the black people around him, the son had known that for him to follow in his footsteps would delight his father as nothing else on earth could. That purpose had dominated his training years and had not been recognized for what it was until the night that his father's death had sent his life crashing about him.

Then he thought of Kay. She had been wiser than he, for she had realized that only the compulsion of love for Christ Himself was sufficient cause for the giving of a life in service for Him. Her life had been centered in Andy, just as his was in his father, and she knew that was not enough. A wave of tenderness toward her swept over him. How brave she had been to face that decision alone and to honestly accept the answer regardless of the cost! He knew that he loved her now as he had never loved her before, knew that if his father were still alive, the love between them would have to take second place to the love he bore Kay. And he knew that was right, and his father would acknowledge it so.

He smiled wryly and thought of psychology class. "I guess I'm just beginning to grow up," he said. "Dr. Schoen would say I've had a 'father complex.' "

Whatever place those two, his father and Kay, had wrongfully occupied in his life, they were as they should be now. Without having become any less dear to him (in fact, they seemed dearer), the place of supremacy was now given to the One whose he was by right of purchase. He thought of Hester on that long-ago night, and he whispered softly, "Forgive, Lord, all my selfish past. Today I 'feel to let You have what You bought, and I'm not grudging it.' Take me, Lord, and do and make what You will with me."

Through his mind ran the words of a hymn that had been loved by his father, and he realized, as he had not before, whence came the strength that had enabled that father to go victoriously on with his lonely ministry after his dearest earthly companion had been taken from him. He repeated it softly.

> The dearest idol I have known,
> Whate'er that idol be,
> Help me to tear it from its throne
> And worship only Thee.

Then the faces and memories of these dear ones faded into the background. There was only One who stood out clearly, One who stood with outstretched wounded hands, saying, "It is for Me alone that you must choose. Not for love of Kay with her dear charm and her sweetness. Not for the sake of the father and mother who gave their lives in the African jungle. They answered My call to the way I chose for them. You must answer to the way I choose for you. It is you and I alone who must settle this."

He lay quietly with his eyes closed and the sense of the Presence strong upon him. After a time of such apartness from the world that he seemed to float in timeless space, he whispered, "Yes, Lord. Just show me where."

And the Voice answered, "Can you see these other sheep of mine?"

Andy looked then beyond the One who was pleading with him, and saw other forms and faces, black faces, vacant and hopeless; black forms, some needing the help and healing he could give them, and all needing the Saviour whom he represented. Behind them all was another face with piteous, pleading eyes, the face of David, his brother.

Then the Voice spoke again to his soul. "For their sakes, too. Can you not choose?"

He thought of the faded writing in the old ledger, the page that told how Andrew Lewis I had accepted his orders.

> *Yes, He called me and I answered. I said, "Anywhere, Lord."*
> *The promise I made was that I'd go where He sent me.*
> *It's because of His orders, not anything else.*

The first two Andrew Lewises had stayed because God said, "Stay." Each soldier must fight in his own place where his Captain commands. The third Andrew Lewis had his orders to go. He would have to go alone, and when he got to Africa, the big house would be lonely. But he would go gladly and not "grudge" the gift.

He lay in silence, letting the peace of surrender and acceptance flood over him. After awhile he began to pray. His had been a life of prayer. He had prayed before he could speak plainly. He had had devotions with his parents as long as they were together, and since leaving home, he had been faithful in his devotional life. He had prayed over his college studies and over his medical training. He had prayed in desperation when he thought a patient was dying during an operation. But never had he prayed as now, with the sense of his whole being in oneness with God. He was on the mountain alone with his Lord. It was good to be there.

Chapter Twenty-eight

Iт was almost dark when he arose and started down the hill to the car. He felt weak, and there was no struggle left in him. The fog of doubt and uncertainty in which he had been wandering had been dispelled by the Presence of the One who Himself is Light.

He thought of Kay, and knew he must write her again. What a weakling she would think him! He had studied and planned for years to be a medical missionary, then because he had been sad and sick at heart, he had thrown it all aside and planned to stay in America. He had written her of the change in his plans, and probably she had revised her own plans for the future to build again the house of dreams she had knocked over with her courageous announcement that she would not offer God a life that placed another above Him.

She had said she still loved him, Andy Lewis, and always would—just as the first Kate Putney had loved Andrew though she would not go with him to a foreign land. Kay, having seen herself as unworthy to go, would have, when she got his last letter, understood how he felt and, loving him as she did, would have started at once to plan for life together. Now he must write and destroy those dreams again. What a mess he had made for the two of them! Kay should be glad to be rid of such a bungler.

There would be no more deviations from the path, however. His course was set now, and he knew where it led. Life might be lonely and hard. He might come to the end of his way with few visible results of his life of service. He would probably burn out while still young, as his parents had before him. He would not know the companionship of sons and daughters, nor the clasp of a woman's hand in his as they faced their task together. But there would be One who would travel with him and that would be enough.

Then he remembered David, and knew he must go as quickly as possible to his aid. He was sure David was not dead. And he knew with deep conviction that he had not turned aside in his faith. Dr. Andrew Lewis might do that in a moment of weakness, but never David! Wherever he was, he had gone in the hope of serving the Lord there. He might be held as a prisoner, but his witness would be untarnished. The first duty waiting in Africa would be the finding of David.

The visa for which he had been waiting must surely be ready by this time. If so, he would go at once. If Grandpa was willing, they would start home the day after tomorrow. There was now no reason for delay. The boxes and crates were all packed in his room, and as soon as a plane reservation could be secured, he'd be off.

As he drove into the yard, Sid waved at him from the barn lot. Sid had known all during the days when Andy was working at his volunteer task that something was troubling him, and had supposed that it was grief over his loss. He had not liked the thought of a day alone in the woods. That did not seem the road to comfort. But when he heard a whistle again as Andy went toward the house, he smiled in relief. Sid did not know that Andy had said good-bye that afternoon to all hope of ever having such a home as Sid enjoyed with his wife and children. All he knew was that there was peace where there had been strain. Whatever battle there had been, it had been settled right.

After the supper dishes were put away Andy brought out his letter from Roy Allison that Grandpa might read it. There were tears in the old man's eyes when he had finished, but all he said was, "I must pray for David. I hadn't heard the latest. Your father used to write about him. I remember when he was converted. He wouldn't recant. Wherever he is, he needs help."

"That's what I think, Grandpa. And I know you'll understand why I think now that I must get back to the city."

"I sure do. And I'm getting rather anxious to get there myself. Charlie's having a big sale in the store next week and I promised I'd clerk in the hardware department. I'd like to stay to get a look at Grace's face when she sees that new kitchen. But that will be a sight for Sid alone, and we'd better skedaddle. With a wedding and all coming up, you won't have too much time. Those Putney women had better come home and get busy."

Andy did not answer. He knew that he must tell Grandpa that Kay was not going with him, but he would wait until they were on the way home. It would be easier when his eyes had to be kept on the road ahead. Tomorrow he would fill with work and avoid any embarrassing questions. He must leave the old cabin in the same immaculate condition in which he found it. There would be a lot of ripe tomatoes, and he would pick them and have them ready for Grace when she came home. He would fill several baskets with garden produce to take back to Aunt Belle. If there were time, he would go again to the hilltop for an hour or so.

He wrote the letter to Kay that evening. He found it easy to pour out to her the whole story—his grief, his loneliness, his revulsion at the thought of Africa, and the complete relinquishment of all his plans. He told of David's disappearance, and of the shock it was to find that he had gone with the fetish worshipers. Then he told her of the old diary and how, as he read it, the character of the writer became so hidden behind the Lord she loved that he had found himself rising up to follow, not her, but her Lord, and yielding himself to that Lord in a new allegiance.

He told of the hours on the hilltop, and his assurance that the place God had for him was in Africa even though it meant

186

he must go alone. He did not try to make light of the pain it gave him to give up, once more, the prospect of winning her. But he met the issue fairly with sorrow for the pain he had caused her by his indecision, and with the assurance that he could never love another woman. He told her that he had found, as had she, that only love for Christ Himself was a sufficient reason for going, and having found that, he could give up all else rather than disappoint that Christ—he must obey the orders and go back to the Congo. Dearly as he loved her, she must not stand between him and his Lord's command. He closed the letter with a promise that wherever he went, he would always pray for her happiness and hope that some day she might find here in America a place of real service.

It was not yet ten o'clock when he finished and he decided to take the letter into the village. In that way it would be delivered to the Putney farm tomorrow and her father could forward it at once. Perhaps she would have time to answer and bid him Godspeed before he left. Just one more glimpse of her would be a memory to carry with him through the lonesome years. He drove the three miles and back, and the quiet of the starlit night lay like a balm on his soul. He knew that he would sleep better than he had for a month.

Chapter Twenty-nine

ANDY AND GRANDPA WERE REST-
ING on the porch after picking the vegetables the next morning when they saw the mailman stopping at the boxes on the
corner. Knowing that the old man always wanted the news-
paper before he took his nap, Andy sauntered down to pick it
up. He shuffled through the bundle, not expecting a letter and
hoping that the one from Kay would not be there. Having
waited so long to answer, she might surely wait a bit longer.
It would simplify things greatly if she could get his second
letter before she answered the first. When he saw it, he could
hardly believe it. It was too ironical that it should arrive now.

He gave Grandpa the rest of the mail and went out to the
cabin. He wanted to be alone when he read that letter, and to
face whatever it might contain with no one watching him.
In spite of his mountaintop experience it was going to be hard.
Her letter would, he was convinced, have in it her acceptance
of his plan to stay in America. It probably would contain
also some hint of the plans she had been making for their
future together here. And all the while the letter that would
disrupt those new plans was on its way to her.

"For the champion messer-upper of lives, I commend to you
Dr. Andrew Lewis," he said grimly, as he tore it open. "I'm
going to feel like a cur over this, but it has to be done."

He was so sure of what she would say that at first he did
not comprehend the import of her words. When he began
to realize her meaning he stopped, went back to the beginning
and reread it all.

188

Dear Andy:

Your letter caught up with me a week ago. The poor thing was almost worn out. We have really been going so fast that we could hardly keep up with ourselves. I should have answered at once, but I was all in a muddle in my own thinking then, and I didn't want to disturb you any further. You've already had enough to bear. I'm awfully sorry about your dad, Andy. My father wrote us about it. I wanted to come to you and put my arms about you and let you know without any words how sorry I am. I find myself wondering why he had to be taken from you just when he was waiting so eagerly for you to come.

When your letter came, I had a terribly guilty feeling. I thought perhaps it was because of me you felt that way. And Andy, much as I love you, I couldn't *stand* it to have you decide to stay here for my sake. I've so many short-comings of my own that I couldn't possibly take on any-body else's. Then I read the letter again, and I understood it all. Who should understand better? You were in the same category as myself. I was going because of love for you, while you were going because of love for your father. And we both found out that wasn't enough, didn't we? It isn't a strong enough compulsion to carry us through all the separation from home folks and the easy, pleasant life here, and to enable us to endure all the hardships that I can only imagine and that you know by experience.

No, not for one minute do I blame you, Andy. I never could. I know how much courage it took for me to an-nounce my similar decision, and yours will be even harder, for my family would rejoice, I knew, while yours will grieve. They must all understand however that such de-cisions can be only between us and God. And they surely will not criticize. No, I won't judge, but I am truly sorry for you. All your life's plans have been predicated on that one thing, and it is cataclysmic to have to change. My heart aches for you more than I can say.

There's another reason why I'm sorry, Andy. For it means that I've got to change my plans again just when I was all set to surprise you with them.

You see, Andy, I'm going to the Congo! I've had a month of thinking and praying and listening to God speak to me, and it has been a pretty solemn time. I had always thought my life was my own, and I could order it as I pleased. When I faced the fact that I was going to Africa because I loved you and that was not a sufficient reason, I was all set to believe I had no place in the Lord's work. I didn't see how He could want or use a trifler. But He had different plans. I became convinced erelong that the "Hound of Heaven" was after me. I "fled Him," but He caught me and won me, and one night I gave in completely. I knew I had to go, not for your sake, but for His. That's the whole story, Andy.

You can understand now why I didn't answer your letter at once. I couldn't until I had conditioned myself to the new setup. Then one day I realized there was a good reason why that letter came just when it did. If I could go to the Congo knowing that you weren't going, I would have proved my sincerity to even my doubting self! I'd know I was going because I loved the Lord and not because I loved Andy Lewis. (In other words, I wouldn't be chasing you.) Of one thing we are both sure now, aren't we? We know that when we serve Him, we must give Him first place. No lesser thing will do.

But I am going to miss you, my darling! I know it is better to miss you for a few years here than to miss His way, but my childish heart still aches. Ray writes that you and Grandpa are at the farm. Maybe I will get to see you there. I don't *think* I can stand it, but I *know* I can't stand it not to! We are leaving here tonight and flying home. By the time this reaches you, we should be there. Mother is sweet about it all. She knows now that I have to do it, but it is going to be hard on them.

I called Mr. Barnes at the Board office and he was delighted when I told him I was going. Said he had always been sure I would — that often the candidates have such doubts just before going out. He said our visas came. I assumed that you had not written him yet of your change of plans so I said nothing. That's up to you.

Oh, I want to see you and tell you good-bye, yet how can I stand it? After chasing you for eighteen years, it's going to be hard to give you up! I'll never love another man, but I've learned my lesson. The Lord must come first.

Always yours,
Kay

He dropped the letter and covered his face with his hands. It was almost more than he could believe. Only God could have planned it. She was going to Africa thinking he would stay behind, while he himself had just made the same decision. Neither had considered the other. They had put Christ first, turned it all over to Him, and He had led to this. Infinite love had given infinite joy.

He sat up and reached for the letter to reread the last paragraph. Why, she would be at home now, she said. The mailman came to Putney's first. Maybe she had his letter!

He could not wait to go by the road. He started along the short cut through the woods, the path that Hester and Sarah used in the long-ago, and which he and Kay had followed together for eighteen years ever since she was so small that she had to be lifted over the creek. He stopped for a minute to lean against a tree and pray.

"Dear God, thank You! We've both of us stumbled along and made a lot of mistakes, but You've kept Your hand on us and brought us home. Thank You for everything, for my mother and dad and for Grandpa and those other folks back yonder who prayed for us who were to come after them. Thank You for Grandmother Hester who wholly followed the Lord and dared to ask big things, of Him. Help us to be worthy of the great thing that has been done for us. In Jesus' name. Amen."

He went on down the path, and as he turned the corner where it came out of the woods, he could see the Putney house. There was no sign of life and he stood watching through a long hour. He could go to the house, of course, but somehow he did not want this meeting to occur under the eyes of any onlooker. So he waited, leaning against the oak under which the old dog had been buried when they were all children. At last he saw Mr. Putney drive in from the field and stop at the mailbox. He was aggravatingly slow in his progress toward the house, waiting to put the car away, to look in on something in the cow barn, and stopping in the yard to examine the new trees. Eventually, however, he disappeared into the house. Again Andy waited until he was sure she had not arrived. Then, just when he had decided to go home and wait until tomorrow, he saw her coming. She was running through the meadow, her skirts and her hair flying. How often he had seen her come like that when the boys were trying to evade her! This time he did not try to hide. He stepped from the shelter of the trees and opened his arms. In a moment she was there. While he was trying to still the beating of his heart enough that he could speak, she laughed shakily, lifting her head from his shoulder.

"Tried to get away from me, didn't you? You should have known better by this time.!"

"I'll never even try again, Miss Biggety. I'm yours for life!"

Then the lightness vanished. He clasped her closely again and whispered huskily, "The wonder and the glory of it! That He should forgive us and love us and use us, and then give us this besides. 'It is the Lord's doing, and it is marvelous in our eyes.' "

THE END